"Lily," he whisp

Then he was moving. Rafael closed the distance between them in a moment, and there was nothing but noise inside him. A great din, pounding at him and tearing at him and ripping him apart, and his hands shook when he reached to take her by the shoulders.

"What are you doing?"

He saw her lips form the words, read them from her mouth, but he couldn't make sense of them. He only knew that was her voice—*her voice*—the voice he'd never expected to hear again, faintly husky and indisputably Lily's. It was like a sledgehammer through him, inside him. Wrecking him and remaking him at once.

And the scent of her…that indefinable fragrance that was some combination of hand lotion and moisturizer, shampoo and perfume, all rolled together and mixed with the simple truth of her beneath it all. All Lily. His Lily.

She was alive. Or this was a psychotic break. And Rafael didn't give much of a damn which.

He simply hauled her toward him and took her mouth with his.

Aberdeenshire

3176490

Secret Heirs of Billionaires

There are some things money can't buy...

Living life at lightning pace, these magnates are no strangers to stakes at their highest. It seems they've got it all... That is until they find out that there's an unplanned item to add to their list of accomplishments!

Achieved:

1. Successful business empire

2. Beautiful women in their bed

3. *An heir to bear their name...?*

Though every billionaire needs to leave his legacy in safe hands, discovering a secret heir shakes up his carefully orchestrated plan in more ways than one!

Uncover their secrets in:

Unwrapping the Castelli Secret by Caitlin Crews

and, coming December 2015

Brunetti's Secret Son by Maya Blake

Look out for more stories in
The Secret Heirs of Billionaires series in 2016!

millsandboon.co.uk

UNWRAPPING THE CASTELLI SECRET

BY
CAITLIN CREWS

MILLS & BOON

Published in Great Britain 2015
by Mills & Boon, an imprint of Harlequin (UK) Limited,
Eton House, 18-24 Paradise Road, Richmond, Surrey, TW9 1SR

© 2015 Caitlin Crews

ISBN: 978-0-263-24929-3

Harlequin (UK) Limited's policy is to use papers that are natural,
renewable and recyclable products and made from wood grown in
sustainable forests. The logging and manufacturing processes conform
to the legal environmental regulations of the country of origin.

Printed and bound in Spain
by CPI, Barcelona

USA TODAY bestseller and RITA® Award-nominated author **Caitlin Crews** loves writing romance. She teaches her favourite romance novels in creative writing classes at places like UCLA Extension's prestigious Writers' Programme, where she finally gets to utilise the MA and PhD in English Literature she received from the University of York in England. She currently lives in California, with her very own hero and too many pets. Visit her at caitlincrews.com.

Books by Caitlin Crews

Mills & Boon Modern Romance

At the Count's Bidding
Undone by the Sultan's Touch
Not Just the Boss's Plaything
A Devil in Disguise
In Defiance of Duty
The Replacement Wife
Princess from the Past

The Chatsfield

Greek's Last Redemption
Traded to the Desert Sheikh

Scandalous Sheikh Brides

Protecting the Desert Heir

Vows of Convenience

His for Revenge
His for a Price

Royal and Ruthless

A Royal without Rules

Scandal in the Spotlight

No More Sweet Surrender
Heiress Behind the Headlines

Visit the Author Profile page
at millsandboon.co.uk for more titles.

CHAPTER ONE

RAFAEL CASTELLI WAS entirely too familiar with ghosts.

He'd seen them everywhere in those first dark months following the accident. Every woman with anything resembling strawberry blond hair was his Lily in a certain light. A hint of her scent in a passing crowd, the suggestion of her delicate features across a busy train car, a low, faintly hoarse bit of feminine laughter in a packed restaurant. All Lily for a heart-stopping instant of wild recognition—and hope.

Always that delirious scrap of hope, as desperate as it was doomed.

He'd once chased a woman halfway across London before he'd realized that she wasn't Lily. That she couldn't have been Lily. His stepsister had died in that terrible crash on the rugged California coast north of San Francisco. And despite the fact that her body had never been recovered from the treacherous waters below that rocky cliff, despite the fact no one had ever found any proof that she'd died in the fire that had burned her car to ash, nothing, not tricks of light or three a.m. conspiracy theories or his own despairing heart playing games with him, could change that.

It had been five years. Lily was gone.

He understood, finally, that they weren't ghosts at all, these flashing glimpses of what might have been. They were his bitter, consuming regret mapped onto a hundred strangers, and none of them the woman he wanted.

But this ghost was different.

And the last, Rafael vowed as a deep, black fury surged through him. Five years was long enough to grieve what had never been, thanks to his own selfishness. More than long enough. It was time to move on.

It was a December late afternoon in Charlottesville, Virginia, a picturesque American university town nestled at the foot of the Blue Ridge Mountains, some three hours by car from Washington, DC, and a world away from his native Italy. Rafael had made the trip from the nation's capital by helicopter today, the better to tour the region's vineyards from above with an eye toward expanding the global reach of the Castelli family's historic wine business. As acting CEO—because his ailing father's immense pride did not allow for an official transfer of leadership to Rafael or his younger brother, Luca, while the old man still drew breath, which was as unsurprising as it was irritating—Rafael had taken many such trips in the past few years. Portugal. South Africa. Chile.

This latest trip to the central Virginia wine region was more of the same. The late-afternoon stop in self-consciously charming Charlottesville en route to a later dinner event with one of the local wine associations was the typical excursion to help promote the charm of the area. Rafael had expected it and in truth, the bustle of the holiday season made the entire town feel like an interactive Christmas card.

It was not unpleasant, he'd thought as they'd walked the outdoor mall, though he had never much cared for the holiday frenzy. Carolers were strewn along the pedestrianized street, their voices mingling and competing in the crisp air. Shoppers milled in and out of the brightly lit shops beneath festive lights and around clusters of street vendors hawking their wares, and Rafael's small group had ducked inside one of the cafés for strong local coffee to ward off the cold. And to battle any traces of jet lag, no doubt. Rafael had made his order a triple shot of espresso, *per piacere*.

And then he'd seen *her*.

The woman moved like poetry against the falling dark, the particular rhythm of her stride chiming deep inside him even though he knew better, drowning out the barrage of Christmas carols assaulting him from the café's overloud sound system.

It had been five years, but Rafael knew that walk in an instant. He knew the swing of those hips and the stretch of those legs. That irresistible roll as she strode past the window where he stood. He caught the flash of her cheek, nothing more.

But that *walk*.

This must stop, he ordered himself coldly. *Lily is dead.*

"Are you all right, Mr. Castelli?" the local wine association host asked worriedly from beside him. His brother, Luca, here in his capacity as global marketing director of Castelli Wine, was too busy on his mobile to do more then frown distractedly in Rafael's direction.

"I will be fine," Rafael gritted out. "Excuse me for a moment."

And he stalked out of the café, pushing his way through the milling holiday crowds and into the waning light.

For a moment, he thought he'd lost her, and he knew that was the best possible outcome of this tired old madness—but then he saw her again, moving on the far side of the mall with that gait that recalled Lily like a shout across the busy street, and that dark current of pure rage sparked in him all over again.

It wasn't Lily. It was never Lily. And yet every time this

happened, Rafael raced after the poor stranger who looked a bit too much like his memories and made a goddamned fool of himself.

"This will be the last time you indulge this weakness," he muttered to himself, and then he set out after this latest incarnation of the woman he knew—*he knew*—he'd never see again.

One more time to stamp out the last spark of that nasty little flame of hope that still refused to die. One last time to prove what he already knew: Lily was gone, she was never coming back, and he would never, ever see her equal.

And maybe, just maybe, he wouldn't look for her in all these strangers' faces if he hadn't been such a bastard to her in the first place.

Rafael doubted he'd ever shift the guilt of all he'd done from its usual place, crouched fat and greasy and bristling with malice in the spot where his soul should have been. But tonight, in this charming little town in a part of America he'd never visited before and likely wouldn't visit again, he would lay what he could of his wretched history to rest.

He didn't expect peace. He didn't deserve it. But he was done chasing phantoms.

She will be a stranger. She is always a stranger. And after you confirm that for the hundredth time, you will never doubt it again.

This had to end. He had to end it.

He couldn't see the face of his quarry, only the fine line of her back and the hint of her willowy form as she walked briskly away from him. She was wrapped up against the December chill in a long black coat and a bright scarf, with only hints of honey-colored hair peeking out from beneath the black knit hat she wore tugged low over her ears. Her hands were thrust deep into her pockets. She was weaving her way through the crowds in a manner that suggested she knew exactly where she was going, and she didn't look back.

And the memories rolled through him like waves against the rocks, crashing over him one after the next. Lily, the only woman who'd ever captured him so completely. Lily, whom he'd lost. Lily, his forbidden lover, his secret and dirty passion, whom he'd hidden from the world and then had to mourn as if she was no more than the daughter of his father's fourth wife. As if she had been nothing more to him than that.

He'd hated himself for so long now it was indistinguishable from that grief that never quite left him. That grief that had transformed him—turning him from a too-rich dilettante who'd been content to throw his family money around rather than make any himself into one of the most formidable businessmen in Italy.

That, too, had taken years. It had been another form of penance.

"Inside you is the seed of a far better man," Lily had said to him the last time he'd seen her, after he'd made her come and then made her cry: his specialty. "I know it. But if you keep going the way you're going, you'll kill it off before it ever has a chance to grow."

"You mistake me for someone who *wants* to grow," Rafael had replied with all that confidently lazy indifference he'd had no idea he'd spend the rest of his life hating himself for feeling. "I don't need to be a bloody garden, Lily. I'm happy as I am."

It was one of the last conversations they'd ever had.

His heart was a hard, almost painful drum inside his chest. His breath came like clouds against the deepening night. He tracked her past this novelty shop, that restaurant and a band of singers in period dress singing "Ave Maria" while he drank in *that walk* as if it was a prayer.

As if this time around, after all these years of regret, he could appreciate that it was the last time he'd ever see it.

He followed her as she left the clamor and bright mess of the downtown mall and started down one of the side streets, marveling at her hauntingly familiar silhouette, that figure he could have drawn in his sleep, the sheer perfection of this woman who *was not Lily* yet looked exactly the way he remembered her.

His Lily, stalking off down a foggy San Francisco street, claiming she wanted nothing more than to get the hell away from him and their twisted relationship at last. Back then he'd laughed, so arrogantly certain she'd come back to him the way she always did. The way she'd been coming back to him since the day they'd first crossed that line when she'd been nineteen.

Another tryst in a hall closet, perhaps, with his hand wrapped over her mouth to muffle her cries as they drove each other crazy only feet away from their families. Another stolen night in her bedroom in her mother's stately home in the moneyed hills of Sausalito, tearing each other apart in the stillness of the northern California night, hands in fists and teeth clenched against the pillows. A hotel room here, a stolen moment in the gardening shed of a summer rental there—all so tawdry, now, in his recollection. All so stupid and wasteful. But then, he'd been so certain there would always be *another*.

His mobile vibrated in his pocket; the assistant he'd left back in that café, he assumed, wondering where in the hell Rafael was. Or perhaps even his brother, Luca, irritated by Rafael's absence when there was work to be done. Either way, he ignored it.

The afternoon was falling fast into evening and Rafael was a different man now than the one he'd been five years ago. He had responsibilities these days; he welcomed them. He couldn't simply chase women across cities the way he had in his youth, though back then, of course, he'd done such things for entirely different reasons. Gluttony, not guilt. He was no longer the inveterate womanizer he'd been then, content to enjoy his questionable relationship with his stepsister in private and all his other and varied conquests in the bright glare of the public eye, never caring if that hurt her.

Never caring about much of anything at all, if he was honest, except keeping himself safe from the claws of emotional entanglements.

This is how it must be, cara, he'd told her with all the offhanded certainty of the shallow, pleasure-seeking fool he'd been then. *No one can ever know what happens between us. They wouldn't understand.*

He was no longer the selfish and twisted young man who had taken a certain delight in carrying on his shameful affair right under the noses of their blended families, simply because he could. Because Lily could not resist him.

The truth was, he'd been equally unable to resist her. A terrible reality he'd only understood when it was much too late.

He'd changed since those days, ghosts or no ghosts. But he was still Rafael Castelli. And this was the very last time he intended to wallow in his guilt. It was time to grow up, accept that he could not change his past no matter how he wished it could be otherwise and stop imagining he saw a dead woman around every corner.

There was no bringing Lily back. There was only living with himself, with what he'd done, as best he could.

The woman slowed that mesmerizing walk of hers, pulling her hand from her pocket and pointing a key fob at a nearby car. The alarm beeped as she stepped into the street and swung around to open the driver's door, and the light from the street lamp just blooming to life above her caught her full in the face—

And hit him like a battle-ax to the gut.

There was a buzzing in his head, a dizzy, lurching thing that almost cut him in half. She jerked against the car door and left it shut, and he had the dim realization that he'd barked out some kind of order. Or had it been her name? She froze where she stood, staring back at him across the hood of a stout little American wagon that could fit six or seven Italian cars, the frigid sidewalk, the whole of the night.

But there was no mistaking who she was.

Lily.

It could be no other. Not with those fine, sculpted cheekbones that perfectly framed her wide, carnal mouth that he'd tasted a thousand times. Not with that perfect heart-shaped face that belonged in a painting in the Uffizi. Her eyes were still that dreamy, sleepy blue that reminded him of California winters. Her hair poked out from beneath her knit hat to tumble down over her shoulders, still that rich summer honey, golds and auburns combined. Her brows were the same shade, arched slightly to give her the look of a seventeenth-century Madonna, and she looked as if she had not aged a single day in five years.

He thought his heart might have dropped from his chest. He felt it plummet to the ground. He took a breath, then another, expecting her features to rearrange themselves into a stranger's as he stared. Expecting to jolt awake somewhere to find this all a dream. Expecting *something*—

He dragged in a deep breath, then let it out. Another. And it was still *her*.

"Lily," he whispered.

Then he was moving. He closed the distance between

them in a moment, and there was nothing but noise inside him. A great din, pounding at him and tearing at him and ripping him apart, and his hands shook when he reached to take her by the shoulders. She made a startled sort of sound, but he was drinking her in, looking for signs. For evidence, like that faint freckle to the left of her mouth, to mark that dent in her cheek when she smiled.

And his hands knew the shape of her shoulders even beneath that thick coat, slender yet strong. He had the sense of that easy fit he remembered, his body and hers, as if they'd been fashioned as puzzle pieces that interlocked. He recognized the way her head fell back, the way her lips parted.

"What are you doing?"

He saw her lips form the words, read them from her mouth, but he couldn't make sense of them. He only knew that was her voice—*her voice*—the voice he'd never expected to hear again, faintly husky and indisputably Lily's. It was like a sledgehammer through him, inside him. Wrecking him and remaking him at once.

And the scent of her, that indefinable fragrance that was some combination of hand lotion and moisturizer, shampoo and perfume, all rolled together and mixed with the simple truth of her beneath it all. All Lily. His Lily.

She was alive. Or this was a psychotic break. And Rafael didn't give much of a damn which.

He simply hauled her toward him and took her mouth with his.

She tasted the way she always had, like light. Like laughter. Like the deepest, darkest cravings and the heaviest need. He was careful at first, tasting her, testing her, his whole body exulting in this impossibility, this thing he'd dreamed a thousand times only to wake up without her, again and again across whole years.

But then, the way it always had, that electric thing that arced between them shifted, blasted into heat lightning and took him whole. So he merely angled his head for that perfect fit he remembered so well and devoured her.

His lost love. His true love.

Finalmente, he thought, his grasp on the English he'd been fluent in since he was a boy eluding him, as if only Italian could make any sense of this. *At last.*

His hands were in her hair, against her cheeks, when she jerked her mouth from his. Their breath mingled into another cloud between them. Her eyes were that impossible blue that had haunted him for half a decade, the color of the crisp San Francisco sky.

"Where the hell have you been?" he grated out at her, sounding more heavily Italian than he had in years. "What the hell is this?"

"Let go of me."

"What?" He didn't understand.

"You seem very upset," she said, in that voice that was etched into his soul, as much a part of him as his own. Her blue eyes were dark with something that looked like panic, which didn't make any kind of sense. "But I need you to let me go. Right now. I promise I won't call the police."

"The police." He couldn't make any sense of this, and only partly because of that great buzzing still in his head. "Why would you call the police?"

Rafael studied her, that lovely face he'd believed he'd never see again. Not in this life. There was heat on her cheeks now, staining them pink. Her mouth was slick from his. But she wasn't melting against him the way she always had before at his slightest touch, and if he wasn't entirely mistaken, the hands she'd lifted to his chest were pushing at him.

At him.

As if, for the first time in almost as long as he'd known her, she was trying to push him away.

Everything in him rebelled, but he let her go. And he more than half expected her to disappear into the darkness drawing tight around them, or a plume of smoke, but she didn't. She held his gaze for a long, cool moment, and then, very deliberately, she wiped her mouth with one hand.

Rafael couldn't define the thing that seared through him then, too bright and much too hot. He only knew it wasn't the least bit civilized.

"What the hell is going on?" he demanded, in the voice he only ever had to use once with his staff. Never twice.

Lily stiffened, but she was still looking at him strangely. Too strangely.

"Please step back." Her voice was low and intense. "We might appear to be alone here, but I assure you, there are all kinds of people who will hear me scream."

"Scream?" He felt something like ill. Or dull. Or—but there were no words for the devastation inside him. There was nothing but need and fury, grief and despair. And that terrible hope he'd held on to all this time, though he'd known it was unhealthy. He'd known it was a weakness he could ill afford. He'd known it was sentimental and morbid.

He'd considered it the least of his penance. But she was alive.

Lily was alive.

"If you assault me again—"

But the fact she was standing here, on a side street in Charlottesville, Virginia, made about as little sense to him as her apparent death had five years ago. He brushed aside whatever she was saying, scowling down at her as the haze began to recede and the shock of this eased. Slightly.

"How did you survive that accident?" he demanded. "How did you end up here, of all places? Where have you been all this time?" Her words caught up with him and he blinked. "Did you say *assault*?"

He hadn't imagined it. She edged away from him, one hand on the side of the car. Her gaze was dark and troubled, and she certainly hadn't greeted him the way he might have expected Lily would—if, of course, he'd ever allowed himself to imagine that she could really still be alive.

Not a ghost this time. The real, flesh-and-blood Lily, standing before him on a cold, dark street.

Even if she was looking at him as if he was a monster.

"Why," he asked, very softly, "are you looking at me as if you don't know who I am?"

She frowned. "Because I don't."

Rafael laughed, though it was a cracked and battered sort of sound.

"You don't," he repeated, as if he was sounding out the words. "You don't know *me*."

"I'm getting in my car now," she told him, too carefully, as if he was some kind of wild animal or psychotic. "You should know that I have my hand on the panic button on my key chain. If you make another move toward me, I will—"

"Lily, stop this," he ordered her, scowling. Or shaking. Or both.

"My name is not Lily." Her frown deepened. "Did you fall and hit your head? It's very icy and they aren't as good about putting down salt as they—"

"I did not hit my head and you are, in fact, Lily Holloway," he gritted out at her, though he wanted to shout it. He wanted to shout down the world. "Do you imagine I wouldn't recognize you? I've known you since you were sixteen."

"My name is Alison Herbert," she replied, eyeing him as if he'd shouted after all, and perhaps in tongues. As he'd done any of the wild, dark things inside his head, none of which could be classified as remotely civilized. "You look like the kind of man people remember, but I'm afraid I don't."

"Lily—"

She moved back and opened the car door beside her, putting it between them. A barrier. A *deliberate* barrier. "I can call nine-one-one for you. Maybe you're hurt."

"Your name is Lily Holloway." He threw it at her, but she didn't react. She only gazed back at him with her too-blue eyes, and he realized he must have knocked that cap from her head when he'd kissed her so wildly, as her hair gleamed in the streetlight's glow, a strawberry blond tangle. He recognized that, too. That indefinable color, only hers. "You grew up outside San Francisco. Your father died when you were a toddler, and your mother married my father, Gianni Castelli, when you were a teenager."

She shook her head, which was better than that blank stare.

"You're afraid of heights, spiders and the stomach flu. You're allergic to shellfish but you love lobster. You graduated from Berkeley with a degree in English literature after writing an absolutely useless thesis on Anglo-Saxon elegies that will serve you in no way whatsoever in any job market. You have a regrettable tattoo of your namesake flower on your right hip and up along your side that you got as an act of drunken rebellion. You were on a spring break trip to Mexico that year and sampled entirely too much tequila. Do you think I'm making these things up to amuse myself?"

"I think you need help," she said with a certain firmness that didn't match his memories of her at all. "Medical help."

"You lost your virginity when you were nineteen," he

threw at her, everything inside him a pitched and mighty roar. "*To me.* You might not remember it, but I bloody well do. I'm the love of your goddamn life!"

CHAPTER TWO

HE WAS HERE.

Five years later, *he* was here. Rafael. *Right here.*

Standing in front of her and looking at her as if she was a ghost, speaking of *love* as if he knew the meaning of the word.

Lily wanted to die on the spot—and for real this time. That kiss still thudded through her, setting her on fire in ways she'd convinced herself were fantasies, not memories, and certainly not the truth. She wanted to throw herself back in his arms, in that same sick, addicted, utterly heedless way she always had. Always. No matter what had happened or not happened between them. She wanted to disappear into him—

But she wasn't that girl anymore. She had other responsibilities now, far bigger ones. Far more important things to think about than her own dizzy pleasure or this destructively self-centered man who had loomed far too large over too much of her life already.

Rafael Castelli was the demon she carried inside her, the dark, selfish thing she fought against every single day of her life. The emblem of her bad behavior, all her terrible choices, her inability to think of anyone or anything but herself. The hurt she'd caused, the pain she'd meted out, whether intentional or not. Rafael was intimately wrapped up in all of that. He was her incentive to live the new life she'd chosen, so far away from the literal wreck of the old. Her boogeyman. The monster beneath her bed in more ways than one.

She hadn't expected that particular metaphor, that vivid memory she'd used as her guiding compass *away* from the person she'd been back when she'd known him, to bloom into life on a random Thursday evening in December. Right here in Charlottesville, where she'd believed she was safe. She'd finally started to *believe* she really could sink into the life she'd made as Alison Herbert. That she could fully become that other, better, new and improved version of herself and never look back.

"Should I go on?" Rafael asked in a tone of voice she couldn't remember him ever using before. Hard, uncompromising. Very nearly ruthless. It should have scared her, and she told herself it did, but what shuddered through her was far more complicated than that as it pooled hot and deep in her belly. Lower. "I've hardly scratched the surface of the things I know about you. I could write a book."

Lily hadn't meant to pretend she didn't know him. Not exactly. She'd been stunned. Frozen in some mix of horror and delight, and then horror *at* that delight. She'd been walking back to her car after running a few errands, had heard a noise behind her on the darkening street as she'd unlocked the car and there he'd been like a dark angel straight out of her nightmares.

Rafael.

She'd hardly had time to take him in. She'd had that flash of recognition—his lean and muscled form that she'd know anywhere in a sleek and extraordinarily well-cut black coat, his gorgeous face a symphony of male beauty from the thick, dark hair he wore cut closer than she remembered it to that mouth of his that had laughed with so little care and then tempted her beyond measure and tormented her beyond imagining—and that stunned, haunted, wondering look in his searing dark gaze.

And then none of that mattered, because he'd been kissing her.

His mouth on hers, after all this time. His taste, his touch. His heat.

Everything had disappeared. The street. The faint music from the outdoor mall in the air around them. The whole city, state, country.

The past five years, gone in a single blast of heat and hunger that had roared through her, blowing apart every single lie she'd been telling herself all this time. That she'd been infatuated with him and nothing more. That time and distance would erode that mad light between them, dimming it into nothing more than girlish silliness. That there was nothing to fear from this man who had been no more than a spoiled little rich boy who'd refused to give up a favorite toy—

The truth was so hot, so demanding, it burned. It told her things she didn't want to know—proved she was as much an addict as she'd ever been, and worse, as her own mother had always been. Clean for five years and that quickly a junkie again. It had shaken her so deeply, so profoundly, that she didn't know what might have happened next—but then she'd remembered.

With a thud so hard it should have toppled her, though it didn't. She'd yanked her mouth from his, appalled at herself.

Because she'd remembered why she couldn't simply fall into this man the way everything inside her yearned to do. Why she couldn't trust herself around him, not even for an instant. Why she had to make him go away again, no matter what it took.

But he was not looking at her as if he had the slightest intention of doing anything of the sort.

"It would be a work of fiction, then," she managed to say now. "If you wrote a book. Because none of those things ever happened to me."

His face changed, then. That haunted expression dimmed, and something far more considering gleamed gold there in the depths of his dark gaze.

"My apologies," he said softly. She felt how dangerous it would be to believe that tone of voice in the goose bumps that prickled all over her, though she kept herself from shivering in reaction. Barely. "Who did you say you were?"

"I'm not sure I want to share my personal information with some ranting madman on the street."

"I am Rafael Castelli," he said, and the way he said his name lilted through her like a song, lyrical and right. Yet another reason to hate herself. "If you don't know me, as you claim, the pertinent details would be these—I am the eldest son of Gianni Castelli and heir to the ancient Castelli fortune. I am acting CEO of the Castelli Wine Company, renowned the world over for my business acumen. I do not hunt women down in the streets. I do not have to do such things."

"Because rich men are so well-known for their reasonable behavior."

"Because if I was in the habit of accosting strange women in the street, it would have been noted before now," he said dryly. "I suspect countries would think twice before letting me cross their borders."

Lily shifted and tried to look the appropriate mixture of blank and confused. "I really think I should call nine-one-one," she murmured. "You're not making any sense."

"There is no need," he said, sounding more Italian than he had a moment ago, which made everything inside her feel edgy. Jagged. That and the tightness of his lean jaw were the only hints she could see of his anger, but she knew it was there. She could feel it. "I will call them myself. You were reported dead five years ago, Lily. Do you really imagine I will be the only person interested in your resurrection?"

"I have to go."

He reached out a hand and wrapped it over the top of her car door as if he intended to keep her there simply by holding the vehicle itself in place. Her curse was that she believed he probably could.

"There is no way in hell I'm letting you out of my sight."

Lily stared back at him, a war raging inside that she fervently hoped wasn't visible on her face. He had to leave. He *had* to. There was no other option. But this was Rafael. He'd never done a single thing he didn't want to do in as long as she'd known him—even back when he'd seemed far more languid and perpetually unbothered than this man who stood before her now, radiating a kind of authority she really didn't want to investigate any further.

"My name is Alison Herbert," she said again. She tipped her head back to meet his gaze, and then she told him the Alison story in all its particulars—save one crucial detail. "I'm originally from Tennessee. I've never been to California and I didn't go to college. I live on a farm outside of town with my friend and landlady, Pepper, who runs a dog boarding and day care facility. I walk the dogs. I play with them. I clean up after them and live in a little cottage there. I have for years. I don't know anything about wine and to be honest, I prefer a good beer." She lifted a shoulder and then dropped it. "I'm not who you think I am."

"Then you will have no problem submitting to a DNA test, to set my mind at ease."

"Why on earth would the state of your mind be of interest to me?"

"Lily has people who care about her." Rafael's shrug seemed far more lethal than hers, a weapon more than a gesture. "There are legal issues. If you are not the woman I would swear you are, prove it."

"Or," she said, distinctly, "I could reach into my pocket and produce the driver's license that proves I'm exactly who I say I am."

"Licenses can be forged. Blood work is much more honest."

"I'm not taking a DNA test because some crazy man on a street thinks I should," Lily snapped. "Listen. I've been more than nice, considering the fact you grabbed me, terrified me and—"

"Was that terror I tasted on your tongue?" His voice was like silk. It slid over her, through her, demolishing what few defenses she had in an instant. Reminding her again why this man was more dangerous to her than heroin. "I rather thought it was something else."

"Step away from this car," she ordered him. She couldn't let herself react. She couldn't let him see that he got under her skin. "I'm going to get in it and drive away, and you're going to let me."

"Not one of those things is going to happen."

"What do you *want*?" she hurled at him. "I told you I don't know who you are!"

"I want the last five years of my life back!" he thundered, his voice a loud, dark thing in the quiet of the street, bouncing back from the walls of the surrounding buildings and making Lily feel flattened. Punctured. "I want you. I've been chasing your ghost for half a decade."

"I'm not—"

"I went to your funeral." The thunder was a stark thing,

then, and far more painful because of it. It punched through her, leaving her winded. Wobbly. "I stood there and played your stepbrother, nothing more. As if my heart hadn't been ripped from my body and battered apart on the rocks where that car went off the road. I didn't sleep for months, for *years*, imagining you losing control of the wheel and plummeting over—" His fine lips pressed together, hard and grim, as he cut himself off. When he spoke again, his voice was hoarse. "Every time I closed my eyes I pictured you screaming."

She would never know how she stood there and stared back at him, as if he was talking about someone else. *He is*, she told herself fiercely. *The Lily Holloway he knew really did die that day. She's never coming back.*

And the Rafael she'd known had never cared about her—or anything—that much. Who was he kidding? She'd been but one of his many women at the time, and she'd accepted that because what else had she known? She'd learned how to lose herself in awful, narcotic men at her mother's knee.

"I'm sorry," she managed to say. "For everyone involved. That sounds horrific."

"Your mother never recovered."

But Lily didn't want to talk about her mother. Her bright and fragile and largely absent mother, who had shivered at the slightest wind, susceptible to every emotional storm that rolled her way. Her mother, who had self-medicated with ever more dangerous combinations of prescription pills, always under the aegis of this or that quack of a doctor.

"Did you know that she died eighteen months ago?" Rafael continued. "That wouldn't have happened if she'd known her daughter was still alive."

That one would leave deep, deep scars, Lily knew. But

she didn't crack. What she felt about her doomed and care-less mother paled in comparison to what she had to keep safe here.

"My mother is in jail," she told him, and she had no idea how she managed to sound so even. "Last I heard she'd found Jesus, for the third time. Maybe this time it'll stick."

"These are all lies." He was too intense. His gaze was too penetrating. She was terribly afraid he could see straight through her, see everything. "What I can't un-derstand is how you imagine you can tell them to my face. You can't really think I'm likely to believe them, can you?"

Lily didn't know what might have happened then. They were at a stalemate and she had no idea how to extricate herself from this—but then she heard voices calling to her from across the street.

Two of Pepper's clients stood there, a married couple who called her Alison and made polite enough conversa-tion while she held herself still, icy with terror, waiting for them to ask after Arlo. But when they did, as they inevi-tably did because this was the South and people still took manners seriously here, she realized there was no need to panic. The man beside her didn't move a muscle. And why would he? It wasn't as if Rafael knew that name. He couldn't possibly know what it meant.

She was something like giddy with her relief when the couple moved on.

"I hope that clears things up for you," she said.

"Because they called you by this assumed name of yours?" Rafael's voice was mild. "Questions only lead to more questions. You've been living here for some time, clearly. You've made yourself part of this community." His expression was harsh. Something like unforgiving. "You had no intention of ever coming home, did you? You were content to let us mourn your death as if it was real."

He'd let go of her car door, and she slammed it shut then, aware of the way his dark eyes narrowed on her as she did. She ignored him, beeping the alarm on and swinging around again, heading back toward the mall. Where there would be lights and people. More people who knew her. More people to put between them and use as a barrier.

"Where are you going?" he asked, not particularly nicely. "Is this what you do now, Lily? You run away? Where will I find you next time—roaming the streets of Paraguay? Mozambique? Under an entirely different assumed name?"

She kept walking, and he fell into step beside her, which wasn't any kind of help. It made her remember far too many things best left shut away inside her. It made her think about things that could only hurt. He matched his athletic stride to hers, the way he always had. He was so close that if she merely leaned a little bit to the left, she could nudge up against his arm, which was the closest they'd ever come to public displays of affection back in the day.

She felt blinded with grief, then, and with that old, sick need that had taken over so much of her life back then. But she kept her eyes straight ahead and told herself it was the cold weather stinging at her eyes, nothing more.

There had to be a way out of this. There had to be a way to get rid of him. She had to keep Arlo safe. That was the only thing that mattered in the past five years and it was the only thing that she could let matter now.

She felt safer once they reached the crowd on the festive mall. Not that she thought Rafael was likely to abduct her or anything that required so much commitment—but if he'd had any thoughts in that direction, it would be a great deal harder surrounded by so many people.

"Are we shopping?" Rafael's voice was sardonic, managing to slice through the noise, the singing. The barricades she'd been erecting inside her as they'd walked. "This reminds me far more of the lonely little heiress I once knew."

"I thought I'd get something hot to drink and get out of the cold for a moment," she said, refusing to react outwardly to what he'd said. Though she had to blink hard to get the red haze to roll back, and it actually hurt to bite her tongue.

She hadn't been a lonely little heiress. There'd been little enough to inherit, first of all, outside her mother's house. But the poor little rich kid in this scenario had been bored, sybaritic party boy Rafael, beloved of C-list actresses, reality television pseudostars and a host of lingerie models. Those had been the women he'd paraded around with in public. Those had been the women he'd brought home with him, the women he'd taunted Lily with on all those terrible family vacations at Lake Tahoe, letting them drape their cosmetically enhanced bodies all over him and then making her admit her jealousy before he'd ease her pain a little with his clever fingers, that awful mouth of his and the things he could do with a few stolen moments against a locked door.

He was a terrible man, she reminded herself fiercely as they ducked out of the way of a kid on a skateboard. He'd been hideous to her, and worse, she'd let him. There was nothing here to be conflicted about. Everything between them had been twisted and wrong. She loathed who she'd been around him. The lies she'd told, the secrets she'd kept. She'd hated that life she'd been trapped in.

She refused to go back to it. She refused to accept that her only fate was to become her sad mother, one way or another. She refused to let the poison of that life, those people, infect Arlo. *She refused.*

Lily didn't wait to see if Rafael was following her—she knew he was, she could *feel* that he was right on her heels like an agent of doom—she simply marched down the mall until she reached her favorite café, then she tossed open the door and walked in.

Straight into another male body.

She heard an Italian curse that Rafael had taught her when she was a teenager—as pretty to the ear as it was profoundly filthy—and she jerked back, only to look up into another set of those dark Castelli eyes.

Damn it.

Luca, younger than Rafael by three years. The quieter, more solid stepbrother, to her recollection, but then, she'd never seen much besides Rafael. Luca looked as if she'd sucker punched him. Lily felt as if she'd sustained the same blow. It might have been possible to convince only Rafael that she was someone else—or so she'd been desperate to believe the whole walk here. But both Castelli brothers? There was no way.

She was completely and utterly screwed.

"Ah, yes," Rafael said from behind her, that sardonic tone of his wrapping around her, far hotter than the heat of the café or the shock in his brother's gaze. "Luca, you remember our late stepsister, Lily. It turns out she's been alive and well and right here in Virginia this whole time. Hale and hearty, as you can see."

"I'm not Lily," she snapped, though she suspected that was more desperate than strategic, especially with both men scowling at her. But there was only one man's scowl she could feel inside her, like acid. "I'm getting tired of telling you that."

Rafael's gaze was a blast of dark fire as he stepped to the side and then steered her out of the way of oncoming foot traffic, there in the café doorway, with a hand on her arm she couldn't shake off fast enough. But perhaps that was even less strategic, she thought, when his lush mouth quirked slightly—very much as if he knew exactly what his touch did to her, even all these years later.

As if he could feel the lick of that fire as well as she could.

He directed his attention to his brother. "Though, you will note, she does appear to be suffering from a convenient case of amnesia."

Which was not a solution, but was the best answer to her current situation, of course.

And it was how Lily decided, right there on the spot in that crowded little café, that amnesia was exactly what she had. In spades.

CHAPTER THREE

"THIS IS IMPOSSIBLE," was all that Luca said, while Lily pretended she wasn't affected by the shock on his face.

"Behold," Rafael answered him darkly, though that hot, furious gaze of his was on Lily, making her skin feel much too hot beneath her winter layers. "I bring you tidings of comfort and joy. Our own Christmas miracle."

"How?" Luca asked. It was the closest to shaken she'd ever heard him.

It made her feel awful. Hollow. But this was no time to indulge that.

The three of them shifted out of the flow of café traffic, over near the row of stools that sat at the window looking over the mall and all its holiday splendor. The Castelli brothers stood there like a six-foot-and-then-some wall of her past, staring at her with entirely too much emotion and intensity. She tried to look unbothered. Or perhaps slightly concerned, if that—the way a stranger would.

"How did she manage to walk away from that crash?" Luca asked. "How did she disappear for five years without a single trace?"

Lily had no intention of telling either one of them how easy that had been. All she'd needed to do was walk away. And then never, ever revisit her past. Never look back. Never revisit any of the people or places she'd known before. All she'd needed was a good enough reason to pretend that she'd had no history whatsoever—and then six weeks into her impetuous, spur-of-the-moment decision, she'd found she had the best reason of all. But how could she explain that to two Italian men who could trace their lineage back centuries?

Even if she'd wanted to explain. Which she didn't.

You can't, she reminded herself sharply. That was the trouble with the Castelli family. Any exposure to them at all and she stopped doing what she knew she should do and started doing whatever it was they wanted, instead.

"Oddly," Rafael replied, in that same dark tone, still studying her though he was clearly speaking to Luca, "she is claiming that she is a different person and that none of that happened to her."

"She is also standing right here in front of you and can speak for herself," Lily said tartly then. "I'm not claiming anything. Your confusion over my identity is very much your problem, not mine. *You* assaulted *me* on a dark street. I think I'm being remarkably indulgent, given the circumstances."

"You assaulted her?" Luca's dark brows edged up his forehead as he shifted his gaze to his brother. "That doesn't sound much like you."

"Of course not." But Rafael still did not look away from Lily as he said that.

Inside, in the warmth and the light of the café, she could see the hints of gold in those dark eyes of his that had once fascinated her beyond measure. And she could feel his mouth against hers again, a wild bright thing in all that December dark. She told herself what moved in her then was a memory, that was all. Nothing more than a memory.

"I don't think—" She almost said *your brother* but caught herself in the nick of time.

Would a stranger to these men know they were brothers at a glance? She thought the family resemblance was
like a shout in a quiet room—unmistakable and obvious.
Their imposing height, their strong shoulders, their rangy,
rampantly masculine forms and all that absurd muscle that
made them look carved to perfection. The thick black hair
that, when left to its own devices, flirted with the ten-
dency to curl.

Luca wore his in a haphazard manner he'd already raked
back from his brow several times as they stood there. Rafael, by contrast, looked like some kind of lethal monk,
with his hair so short and that grim look on his face. But
they shared the same mouth, carnal and full, and she
knew they even laughed in that same captivating, stunning way—using the whole of their bodies as if giving
themselves over to pleasure was why they'd been placed
on this earth.

Not that she could imagine this stark, furious, older
version of Rafael laughing about anything—and she told
herself she felt nothing at that thought. No pang. No sharp
thing in the vicinity of her chest. Nothing at all.

She directed her attention toward Luca. "I don't think
your friend is well."

"That's a nice touch," Rafael said flatly. "'Friend.' Very
convincing. But I am not the one who is in some doubt as
to his identity."

"I'm so glad you're here," Lily continued, still looking
at Luca, though it was almost as if he appeared in silhouette, with Rafael the dark and brooding sun that was the
only thing she could see no matter where she looked. "I'm
not sure, but he might need medical attention."

Rafael said something in a sleek torrent of Italian that
made Luca blink, then nod once, sharply. Clearly Rafael
had issued an order. And it seemed that in this incarna-

tion of the Castelli family, Rafael expected his orders to be followed and, more astonishing by far, they were. Because Luca turned away, toward a man and woman she'd completely failed to notice were sitting on the stools a few feet away watching this interaction with varying degrees of interest, and started talking to them in a manner clearly designed to turn their attention to him.

And off Lily and Rafael.

"I'm going to leave you in your friend's hands now," Lily told Rafael then, in a falsely bright sort of voice that she hoped carried over the shout of the espresso machine and some pop star's whiny rendition of a Christmas carol on the sound system.

Rafael's mouth moved again, another one of those too-hard quirks that felt wired directly to every last nerve in her body. It set them all alight and shivering. "Do you think so?"

"I have a life." She shouldn't have snapped that. It sounded defensive. A true stranger wouldn't be *defensive*, would she? "I have—" She had to be careful. So very careful "—things to do that don't include tending to strange men and their confusion over matters that have nothing to do with me."

"Why did you come here?" he asked, much too quietly, when she could see temper and pain and something far darker in gaze.

Maybe that was why she didn't throw herself out the door. That darkness that she could feel inside her, too. The guilt she couldn't quite shake. But she did deliberately misunderstand him.

"This is my favorite coffee shop in Charlottesville. I was hoping a peppermint mocha might wash away all of that weirdness out in the street, and give you time to sober up."

Amusement lit his dark gaze and it walloped her hard in the gut. So hard she saw stars for a moment.

"Am I drunk?"

"I don't know what you are." She tilted her head slightly. "I don't know *who* you are."

"So you have said."

Lily waved a dismissive hand in the air. "I think this must be a rich-man thing. You think you see someone you know in the street, so you hunt them down and demand that they admit they're that person, despite their insistence—and documented proof—that they're someone else. I'd end up in jail if I tried that—or on a psychiatric ward. But I imagine that's not a concern for someone as wealthy as you are."

"Has my net worth penetrated the shroud of your broken memory?" His voice should have left marks, it was so scathing. "I find that is often the case. It's amazing how many women I've never met can estimate my net worth to the penny."

"You told me you were rich." She used a tone she was quite certain no one had ever used on him before. One that suggested he was extraordinarily dim, though he looked more entertained by that than he did furious. "Not to mention, you're not exactly dressed like a vagrant, are you?"

"When will this performance end?" he asked softly.

"Right now." She straightened. "I'm going home. And I'm not asking you if that's all right with you. I'm informing you. I suggest you get a good night's sleep—maybe then you'll stop seeing things."

"What is amusing about that, Lily, is that tonight is the first time in five years that I haven't seen a ghost when I thought I saw you." He didn't look as if he found that even remotely amusing. She knew she didn't. "You are entirely real and standing right here in front of me, at long last."

She forced a smile. "They say everyone has a twin."

"If I were to open your coat and look beneath your shirt right now, what would I find?" he asked in the same softly menacing way.

"An assault charge," she retorted, her tone brisk. "And a potential jail sentence, God willing."

His mouth shifted into something not quite a smile. "A scarlet lily nestled in a climbing black vine, crawling over your right hip and stretching up your side, perhaps?"

His dark gaze was so intent, so absolutely certain, that it took her breath away. And it was far harder than it should have been to simply stand there. To do nothing. To keep herself from touching her side in wordless acknowledgment, jerking back as if he'd caught her or any of a hundred other little tells that would show him her guilt.

Not that he appeared to be in any doubt about her guilt. Or her identity.

"There are a number of good psychiatrists in the Charlottesville area," she told him when she was certain she could speak without any of that turmoil in her voice. Only the politeness she'd offer any random person she encountered, with a little compassion for someone so obviously nutty. "I'm sure one of them would see you for an emergency session. Your net worth will undoubtedly help with that."

He really smiled then, though it was nothing like the Rafael smiles of old, so bright and carefree he could have lit up the whole of Europe if he'd wanted. This one was hard. Focused. Determined—and still it echoed deep inside her like a touch.

She was so busy telling herself that he didn't affect her and he didn't get to her *at all* that she didn't move out of the way fast enough. She didn't even see the danger until it was too late. His hand was on her too quickly, his fingers brushing over her temple, and Lily didn't know how to react as sensation seared through her.

Would a stranger leap away? Or stand there, frozen in shock and disbelief?

"Get your hand off me right now," she gritted out, going with the frozen option—because that was what she was. Head to toe. She didn't think she could move if she'd wanted to, she was so rooted to the ground in what she told herself was *outrage*. She could feel his touch everywhere. *Everywhere*. Hot and right and perfect. As if all these years later, the merest brush of his fingers was all he had to do to prove that she'd been stumbling around in the cold black-and-white dark without him.

This was heat. *This* was color and light and—

This is dangerous! everything inside her shrieked in belated alarm.

"You got this scar skiing in Tahoe one winter," he murmured, his voice pitched low, as if those were words of love or sex instead of accusation as he traced the tiny mark she'd long since forgotten was there. Up, then down. The effect was narcotic. "You hit a patch of ice and then, shortly after that, a tree. You were lucky you didn't break anything except one ski. You had to walk down the side of the mountain, and you terrified the entire family when you appeared in the chalet, bleeding."

He moved closer, those dark eyes of his intense and moody, focused on that little scar she didn't even see anymore when she looked at herself. And surely the stranger she was pretending to be would have been paralyzed just as she was, then—suspended between the need to run screaming into the street and the desire to stay right where she was. Surely anyone would do the same.

Anyone for whom this man has always been a terrible addiction, a harsh voice inside told her.

But she still didn't move.

"And I had to make the sarcastic remarks of the bored older brother I never was to you," Rafael said gruffly. "Playing it off for our parents. Until later."

Lily blinked. She remembered *later*. He'd used the key she shouldn't have given him to her hotel room and found her in the shower. She could remember it too easily, too well, in too much detail. The steam. The sting of the hot water against her chilled skin. Rafael shouldering his way into the glassed-in little cubicle still fully dressed, his mouth uncharacteristically grim and a harsh light in his beautiful eyes.

Then his mouth had been on hers, and she'd wrapped herself around him, melting into him the way she always had. His hands had slicked over the curve of her hips, that damned tattoo she'd claimed she hated and he'd claimed he loved, until he'd simply dispensed with his wet trousers, picked her up and surged deep inside her with one slick, sure thrust.

"Don't ever scare me like that again," he'd muttered into her hair, and then he'd pounded them both into a wild, screaming oblivion. Then he'd carried her out of the shower, laid her out on the hotel bed and done it all over again. Twice.

She'd found that desperately romantic at the time, but then, she'd been a pathetic twenty-two-year-old under this man's spell that winter. Now, she told herself firmly, it was nothing more than another bad memory wrapped up in too much sex she shouldn't have been having with a man she never, ever should have touched.

"That is a very disturbing story with some deeply troubling family dynamics," she said now, batting his hand away from her face. "But it still doesn't make me this other woman, no matter how many stories you tell to convince yourself otherwise."

"Then you must take a DNA test and prove it."

She rolled her eyes. "Thank you, but I'll pass."

"It wasn't a suggestion."

"It was an order?" She laughed then, and kept it light somehow. She could see Luca looking over, and those people with him, and knew she'd stayed too long. She had to walk away, because a stranger would have done that long ago. "I'm sure you're used to giving lots of orders. But that doesn't have anything to do with me, either." She caught Luca's gaze and forced a tight smile. "He's all yours."

Lily started for the door then, and she expected Rafael to stop her. She expected a hand on her arm, or worse, and she told herself she *absolutely did not* feel anything like a letdown when nothing happened. She threw the door open and then, though she knew better, she couldn't help looking back over her shoulder.

Rafael stood where she'd left him and watched her, dark and beautiful and harsher than she'd ever seen him before. She repressed a shiver and told herself it was the December evening. Not him.

"*Mi appartieni,*" he said, soft and fierce at once. And she understood that little scrap of Italian. He'd taught it to her a long time ago. *You belong to me.*

Lily sniffed, the cold night in her hair and slapping at her cheeks.

"I don't speak Spanish," she managed to say, though her voice was rougher than it should have been had she really not been able to tell the difference between Spanish and Italian. "I'm not her."

Once she was gone, swallowed back up by the thick Virginia night, everything inside Rafael went still. Quiet. From that insane buzzing when he'd realized it was really, truly her to a sharp clarity he couldn't recall ever feeling before.

His brother and their wine association host were talking, and his assistant was trying to show him something business related on his mobile screen, but Rafael simply slashed a hand through the air and they all subsided.

"There is a kennel outside of town run by someone called Pepper," he told his aide in rapid-fire Italian. "Find it." He shifted his gaze to Luca. "Call Father's personal doctor and ask him how a person could have walked away from that accident five years ago and what kind of head injuries she might have sustained when she did."

"Do you believe she truly has amnesia?" Luca asked. "It sounds like something out of a soap opera. But it is Lily, certainly."

"There is no doubt about that whatsoever," Rafael agreed. He'd known it was Lily the moment he'd seen her walk past this window. All the rest was mere confirmation of a truth he already knew, and the taste of her in his mouth after much too long.

Luca stared at him for a moment. "Your grief at her death was extreme. I am closer to her in age and I was less affected. You altered the whole of your life afterward, very much as if…"

Rafael only stared back at his younger brother, brows raised in challenge, daring him to finish that sentence. He didn't know what Luca saw on his face, but the younger man only nodded, very wisely checked what looked like a smile and then pulled out his mobile.

It took very little time to get the answers he'd requested, dispatch the wine association woman off to tender their apologies to their would-be dinner companions and set out to find Lily in the car his assistant had waiting for them a block outside the pedestrianized area.

"If she is faking this memory loss," Luca said as he lounged in the back of the sleek vehicle with Rafael, "she might be gone already. Why would she stay? She obviously didn't want to be found."

Rafael kept his gaze out the window as the car slipped through the streets and then out into the fields, barren this time of year and gleaming beneath a pale moon. He didn't think Lily would have moved on yet, with that same gut-deep certainty that told him she was faking this whole thing. She'd been so adamant that she was this other woman, this *Alison*. He thought the stubborn girl he'd known was far more likely to dig in her heels and brave it out than turn and run—

But the truth is, you don't know her at all, a dark little voice inside him whispered harshly. *Because the girl you knew would never have walked away from you.*

"We have a responsibility, as the closest thing Lily has left to any kind of family, to determine that she is not suffering from some kind of post-traumatic stress brought on by the accident," Rafael said. "At the very least."

The words came so easily to him, when deep down, he knew they were excuses. *Lily was alive.* That meant he would do whatever he must to claim her the way he should have done five years ago.

But he didn't want to say that to his brother. Not yet.

It was all for the best, he thought, that Luca did not respond.

The roads were emptier the farther they got from the center of Charlottesville, and the land on either side of the car was beautiful. Stark trees with their empty branches rose over fields still white from the last snow. This was rich, arable land, Rafael knew. Lily had always loved the extensive Castelli vineyards in the northern Sonoma Valley. Perhaps it should not surprise him that she'd found a place to live that was reminiscent. Gnarled vines and plump grapes had been a part of her life since she'd been sixteen and not at all pleased her mother was remarrying.

And even less pleased with him.

He could remember it all so clearly as the car made its way through the frozen Virginia fields. Rafael had been twenty-two. Their parents had gathered them together in the sprawling château that served as the Castelli Wine hub of operation and foremost winery in the States.

And Francine Holloway had been exactly what they'd expected. Beautiful, if fragile and fine featured, with masses of white-blond hair and sky-blue eyes. She'd trembled like a high-strung Thoroughbred and spoken in the kind of soft, high-pitched voice that made a certain sort of man lean in closer. Rafael's father was precisely that type. He'd loved nothing more than wading in and solving the problems of broken, pretty things like Francine—a preference that dated back to Rafael's mother, who had spent many years, before and after the divorce, institutionalized in a high-end facility in Switzerland.

Rafael had expected the teenaged daughter to be much the same as the mother, especially with such a wispy, feminine name. But this Lily was fierce. Laughably so, he'd thought, as she'd sat stiffly on an overwrought settee in the formal sitting room at the château and scowled through the introductions.

"You do not appear to hold our parents' mutual happiness foremost in your heart," he'd teased her after an endless dinner during which his father had delivered the sort of speeches that might have been moving had Francine not been the old man's fourth wife, and had Rafael not heard them all before.

"I don't care about our parents' happiness at all," she'd retorted, without looking at him. That had been different. Most girls her age took one look at him and melted into shallow little puddles at his feet. That hadn't been arrogance on his part. It had been pure, glorious fact—though he'd been, by his own estimation, far too worldly and sophisticated to sample the charms of such young, silly creatures. This one, apparently immune, had sniffed, her gaze trained somewhere far off in the distance through the great windows. "Which is about how much they care about ours, I imagine."

"I'm sure they care," Rafael had said, thinking he might soothe her girlish fears with the wisdom of his years. "You have to give them a chance to get over how perfect they imagine they are for each other so they can pay attention to their lives again."

But Lily had turned to face him, that heart-shaped face of hers still faintly rounded with youth, those impossible eyes scornful. She'd been dressed in a perfectly appropriate sundress that showed nothing untoward at all and yet there had been something about the way she'd worn the masses of her strawberry blond hair tumbling in every direction, or the fact that her shoulders were far too smooth, that had made Rafael wonder what it would be like to touch her—

He'd been horrified.

"I don't need a big brother," she'd told him baldly, compounding his shock at the direction of his own thoughts. "I don't want the unsolicited advice, especially from someone like you."

"Someone like me?"

"Someone who dates people purely to end up on tabloid television shows, which I'm sure keeps you super relevant in the world of the vapid and the rich. Congrats. And I don't need you to fill me in on my mother's ridiculous patterns. I know them all too well, thank you. Your father is the latest in a long line of white knights who never quite manage to save her. It won't last."

She'd turned back to the view, her manner clearly dismissive, but Rafael had not been accustomed to being dismissed. Especially not by teenage girls who were usually much more apt to follow him around and giggle. He hadn't been able to imagine Lily Holloway doing anything of the sort.

"Ah," he'd said, "but I think you'll find it will last."

She'd heaved a sigh but hadn't looked at him again. "My mother's relationships have the shelf life of organic produce. Just FYI."

"But my father is a Castelli." He'd only shrugged when she'd looked back at him then, her nose wrinkled as if he was more than a little distasteful. "We always get what we want, Lily. Always."

Sitting in the back of his car as it turned from the main country road and headed down a smaller, private lane lit with quiet lights shaped like lanterns, Rafael still didn't know why he'd said that. Had he known then? Had he suspected what was to come? Lily had hated him openly and happily for three more years, which had distinguished her from pretty much every other woman on the planet. She'd insulted him, laughed at him, mocked him and dismissed him a thousand times. He'd told himself she was obnoxious. He'd told himself she was jealous.

"She is unbearable," he'd growled at Luca once, when Lily had spent an evening singing pointed old songs at him and his date.

"But your date really is acting her shoe size instead of her age," his brother had replied, with a lazy grin. "Lily's not wrong."

And then had come that fateful New Year's Eve party at the château in Sonoma. Rafael had perhaps had too much of the Castelli champagne. He'd long told himself he was simply drunk and she must have been, too, but he'd had five long years thinking she was dead and gone to admit to himself that he hadn't been anything like drunk. He'd known exactly what he'd been doing when she'd sauntered past him in the upstairs hall of the family wing, in what he'd openly called "hooker shoes" earlier and a dress he'd thought trashily short. Her hair had been tumbling down the way it always had back then, sliding this way and that. The scent of her, a sugared heat, had been maddening.

"If you're looking for *Calliope*," she'd said, and had managed to make his then girlfriend's ridiculous name sound like an insult, "she's probably in the nursery with the other children. Your father hired a babysitting service." She'd smirked at him. "He was obviously expecting you."

Rafael had known that the last thing in the world he should have done was reach over, slide his palm around her neck and yank that smart mouth to his. Of course he'd known. He'd imagined he would kiss her, she would punch him and he would laugh at her and tell her that if she wasn't angling to take Calliope's place, she should keep quiet.

But one touch of her mouth with his, and everything had changed.

Everything.

And you ruined it, he told himself savagely then, as an old farmhouse came into view at the end of the lane. *Because that is what you do.*

The car pulled up in front of the bright old house and was promptly surrounded by a pack of baying dogs. Rafael climbed out of the car as a silver-haired woman charged out of the house and straight toward them in some misguided attempt to corral her charges.

But despite the barking and howling and general din,

Rafael knew it the moment Lily appeared on the step behind the older woman, as if everything else fell quiet. He drank her in. Again. She was no longer wearing her coat and scarf, and he couldn't keep himself from tracing the fine, elegant lines of that willowy body of hers. Her jeans were snug, making his mouth water, and the long-sleeved shirt she wore hugged her breasts and made him realize how hard and hungry he was for her—even in this sea of animals.

And even if she looked horrified to see him.

"This is stalking!" she threw at him from her place on the steps. "You can't hunt me down at my home. You don't have any right!"

Before Rafael could reply, a streaking shape shoved past her and would have hurtled itself down the steps and into the chaos had Lily not reached out and grabbed it.

Not an it. A boy. A small one.

"I told you to stay inside no matter what," Lily told him sharply.

"Arlo is barely five," the older woman said from somewhere off to the side where, Rafael was dimly aware, she'd managed to move all the dogs into a fenced-off pen. But he couldn't look away from Lily. And the boy. "He doesn't get 'no matter what.'"

The little boy looked at the older woman, then angled his head back to look up at Lily, who still held him by the collar of his shirt.

"Sorry, Mama," he said, angelically, and then he grinned up at her.

It was a mischievous grin. It was filled with light and laughter and the expectation that his sins would be forgiven in an instant, simply because he'd wielded it. Rafael knew that smile well. He'd seen a version of it on his brother's face throughout Luca's whole life. He'd seen it in his own mirror a thousand times more.

His heart stopped beating. Then started again with a deafening, terrible kick that should have knocked him to the ground. He couldn't quite understand why it hadn't.

"You don't have the right to be here," Lily said again, her cheeks flushed and her eyes glittering, and Rafael didn't know how he could want her this badly. He'd never understood it. And it was back as if she'd never been gone, a yearning so deep it was like an ache inside him.

But it didn't matter any longer. None of that mattered. The little boy didn't resemble the fair woman he'd called Mama at all. He had Rafael's dark curls and the Castelli dark eyes. He looked like every picture Rafael had ever seen of himself as a child, scattered all over the ancestral Castelli home in northern Italy.

"Are you so certain I don't have the right to be here, *Alison*?" Rafael asked, amazed he could speak when everything inside him was a shout again, long and loud and drowning out the world. "Because unless I am very much mistaken, that appears to be my son."

CHAPTER FOUR

THEY LANDED AT the private Castelli airstrip, high in the far reaches of northern Italy in the shadow of the towering Dolomites, just after dawn the following morning. Daylight was only beginning to stretch out pink and crystalline over the jagged spires and craggy, snowcapped heights of the sharply imposing mountains on either side of the narrow valley. Lily stared out of the window as the plane taxied down the scenic little runway, feeling as if someone had kicked her in the stomach.

She'd never imagined she'd see this place again. For years now she'd told herself she didn't want to see it or anything else the Castellis owned again, including those wine bottles with their distinctive labels in the liquor store—yet there was no mistaking the way her heart leaped as the private jet touched down. There was no denying the fact that this felt a whole lot more like a homecoming than it should. Certainly more than was safe.

Last night had been the second-worst night of her life, all things considered.

She'd known on the long drive home from Charlottesville after she'd left Rafael in that café that he wasn't likely to simply disappear. Not Rafael. He might have been spoiled rotten when she'd known him, a being created entirely out of wealth and privilege and more than happy to exploit both to serve his own ends—but he'd always gotten what he'd wanted. Lily being but one in a long line of things he'd taken because he could.

She'd sped along the dark country roads, hardly seeing the cold winter beauty of this place she'd come to call home. Lost in that kiss again. Lost in *him*. If it had been only her, she would have left then and there. Just kept on driving until she became someone else, somewhere else. She'd done it before. She knew exactly what it took to disappear without a trace.

But she wasn't twenty-three and desperate any longer, and there was Arlo now. Her beautiful, magical little boy. She'd turned it over and over in her head all throughout that drive, but she couldn't see how she could legitimately uproot Arlo and make *him* act like he was in the witness protection program for the rest of his life simply because *she* didn't want to deal with his father.

His father.

It still made her shiver to think of Rafael that way.

She could remember when she'd confirmed she was pregnant as vividly as if it had happened last night out there on those lonely country roads. She'd been dead for six weeks by then. Every day that she'd stayed away from her old life had been easier than the one before, because it was that much harder to go back. Too much time had passed. A day or two's worth of confusion, maybe a couple of weeks—she could have explained that away in the wake of her accident. But six whole weeks without so much as a scratch on her? That indicated intent, she'd thought. They'd know she'd disappeared deliberately.

Lily had looked at the coverage of her car accident from a library computer in Texas once, early on, but that had been a mistake she hadn't repeated. Seeing the people that she'd loved grieving for her loss had made her feel like the lowest kind of worm. A truly despicable human being. How could she walk back into their lives having caused them so much pain? What could she say?

Oh, sorry, everybody, I thought I wanted to make a clean break from all this and making you think I died horribly in that accident seemed like a good idea at the time...

After a few weeks of feeling strangely thick and deeply ill in turns, she'd taken a pregnancy test in a truck stop bathroom near the Missouri-Arkansas border. She could remember every detail of that winter morning. The sound of the big rigs outside. The chill in the air that seemed to have crept deep into her bones in the unheated little stall. The way her stomach had sunk down to the dirty floor and stayed there as she'd stared in an unmitigated horror at the positive test in her hand for what might have been whole years.

There'd been no going back. She'd understood several things with a rush of clarity in that badly lit bathroom in the middle of nowhere. That, despite everything—like the memorial service they'd held for her in Sausalito a few weeks after the accident—she'd believed until that moment that she might go back someday. That she'd pretended it wasn't an option for her while holding it there in reserve, tucked away in the back of her mind.

And that the fact she'd been pregnant with Rafael's child meant that door was forever closed to her.

It had been bad enough that she'd had a relationship with Rafael for all those years, no matter who else he'd been seeing and no matter how badly their families would have reacted to it if they'd known. It had been twisted and it had been wrong, given the fact her mother had insisted on referring to Rafael and Luca as *your big brothers* at every opportunity. How could she bring a baby into that gnarled, sick mess? Not to mention, she'd had no idea how Rafael might behave in the face of real adversity. Would he deny he was the father? Would he order her to terminate the pregnancy?

How had her life come to this? she'd wondered. That she'd felt she had no option but to walk away from everything she knew—only to discover that she'd made a new life with a man she obviously didn't know at all if she had so little idea how he might react or what he might do.

She'd vowed then and there that she would raise this child better than this squalid little beginning in a truck stop bathroom. That she would give her baby a fresh start in a new place where her sick need for Rafael—like her own mother's varied addictions that had marked Lily's own life so deeply—was no longer a factor. Where the child could come first, and not her—the very opposite of how she'd been raised.

And she'd done a good job sticking to all of those vows, she'd thought last night as she'd pulled up in front of the farmhouse. Arlo had come hurtling outside as she'd parked, heedless of the wintry weather the way he always was—as excited and bouncy as the dogs who romped along with him. She'd caught his hot and squirmy little body against hers in a hard hug, and had poured all her regrets and apologies into the way she squeezed him tight until he wriggled free.

Because she'd known it was only a matter of time, and sure enough, they hadn't even started their usual nightly dinner with Pepper when the car had pulled up outside. She'd tried to hold back the inevitable that little bit longer—but there had been no stopping it. On some level, she'd known that since she'd looked up and seen Rafael on the street.

And it had been even worse than she'd imagined.

She'd known that Arlo took after his father, of course, but it had been one thing to know it and another entirely to *see* it in the flesh. It had made her heart flip over in her chest and her eyes prickle with heat...

But then Rafael had turned that frozen, astonished glare on her, his eyes so dark they'd made the deep December night around him seem bright by comparison. And while it hadn't been as terrifying or dramatic as that car crash five years ago, Lily had known that it amounted to the same thing.

One life was over. A new one was beginning—whether she wanted it or not.

It had all been very cut-and-dried. There had been no mistaking the connection between father and son. It was written on both their faces, as obvious as the sun. And though Lily had valiantly stuck to her Alison story, which included a part about a drug dealer boyfriend who'd conveniently died after helping make Arlo, Pepper had been involved in the conversation this time.

Pepper, who'd confirmed that yes, Alison had that exact tattoo that Rafael mentioned, which had made Rafael's mouth curve in a way that had in turn made Lily's heart kick at her. And no, Pepper had said when pressed, she'd never met a single person from Alison's life before Charlottesville. And therefore, no, there was no corroboration to any of the Alison stories at all.

Only what Lily had told her.

"I told you what I know," Lily had said at that point, and she'd worried that the lies were like tattoos she wore on her face. That they were that bright, that indelible. "Everything I know."

Lily had been involved in a serious car accident on the winding California coastal road five years ago, Rafael had said—for Pepper's benefit, presumably—and Luca had confirmed. Her body had never been found. Now they knew why.

"How can you explain the fact that I'm here and don't remember you?" Lily had demanded, as Pepper had stared at her from across the table as if looking for the truth on her face. Or those terrible tattoos Lily was sure she could *feel* stamped across her cheekbones. "This doesn't make any sense."

"I don't know how a woman could go over the side of a cliff on the Sonoma Coast and yet turn up unharmed five years later on the other side of the country, with a memory of a completely different woman's life and a child who is inarguably mine," Rafael had said, a seething fury in his voice and in his eyes though he'd sat at Pepper's table so easily. So calmly. As if he was a friend instead of a foe— but Lily couldn't accuse him of that if she was pretending she didn't know him, could she? Maybe a stranger wouldn't be able to read him as well as she could. "I only know that you are the same woman. That means it happened, whether it makes sense or not."

And the truth was, there had been no need to trot out all the old pictures Rafael apparently kept cached on his mobile and ready to show, because this game had ended the moment Pepper had seen Rafael next to his son.

His son.

"This is a good thing," Pepper had whispered fiercely, hugging Lily as the Castelli brothers had led them away from the only home Arlo had ever known. "Everyone should know who they really are, honey. And that little boy needs his father."

Lily had questioned whether anybody needed Rafael Castelli, especially the child she had no intention of allowing him to corrupt, but she'd known better than to say that out loud. And it had been out of her hands. She'd been utterly outmaneuvered. The only card she could possibly have played was a demand for a blood test as some kind of stalling tactic—but to what end? She already knew what it would say.

And anyway, Rafael had anticipated that move.

"We will take the helicopter back to Washington, DC," he'd told her in that cool way of his, at such odds with her memories of his tempestuousness and that ferocious gleam in his gaze. "Where a suitably discreet doctor is waiting to perform the necessary blood work. We will know the whole biological truth before we land in Italy. If there has been some mistake, I promise you that the Castelli family will see to it that you and your son have a lovely holiday in Italy before we return you back here to your home, safe and sound."

"Wonderful," she'd retorted, baring her teeth in some approximation of a smile. "I've always wanted to see Venice. Before it sinks."

The jet rolled to a stop on the Castelli airfield, jerking her back into the wholly unwelcome present. Arlo was already bouncing up and down in his seat beside her with his usual boundless energy, and she could hardly blame him for taking off at a dead run once the plane's door opened and the cold, crisp mountain air poured in.

She took her time, but there was only so much dawdling she could do before she, too, had to step off the plane and climb down the metal steps. Putting her well and truly back in Italy. The truth of that felt like a blow. And it was even more beautiful here than she remembered it, so stunning it actually hurt—the soaring heights of the Alps dressed up in their winter whites, the blue sky with hints of pink and coral from the exultant dawn still fading away as she watched—and the man who waited for her at the foot of the steps as darkly gorgeous and even more dangerous than the view.

Rafael slid his mobile into his pocket as she stepped onto the solid, frozen ground beside him. Lily refused to look at him, and then despaired of herself if something so small and pointless was her only potential rebellion. *Pathetic.* She could feel her heart in her throat, and for the first time in her entire life, thought it was within the realm of possibility that she might faint.

Don't you dare! she snapped at herself. And not because fainting was a weakness, though it likely was and she didn't want to show any weakness here. But because she knew Rafael would catch her and the very last place she needed to be, ever again, was in his arms.

She kept her gaze trained on Arlo, who was chasing his uncle up and down the otherwise empty runway, kept as it was for the family's use alone. A gleaming black Range Rover waited at a discreet distance, poised to sweep them all down to the grand old house that lounged across several acres at one end of the crystal-blue mountain-rimmed alpine lake the locals called Lago di Lacrime.

Lake of Tears, Lily thought darkly, glaring in the direction where she knew the lake waited, out of sight behind the nearest wall of alpine rock. *How appropriate.*

"I'm afraid the results of the blood tests are in and allow no further room for debate," Rafael told her then, his voice quietly triumphant in a way that made her skin feel shrunken down too tight against her own bones. "You are Lily Holloway. And Arlo is very much our son."

She should feel something big, Lily thought then. Panic. Desperation. Even the polar opposite of that—a pervasive sense of relief, perhaps. Or perhaps of homecoming, after all these years of hiding.

But what she felt, instead, was profoundly sad.

Our son, he'd said, as if they were like other people. As if that was a possibility. As if they hadn't ruined each other, down deep into their cores, so comprehensively that even the past five years hadn't healed it or changed it at all.

Lily didn't think anything ever could.

They stood there together in one of the most gorgeous and remote spots in the world. The thrust of the fierce mountains was exhilarating, the sky bluer by the moment while the crisp wind danced through her hair and moved over her face like a caress, and it was beautiful. It was more than beautiful. And yet all she could see was the dark, twisted past that had brought them here. Her terrible addiction to him and his profound selfishness. Their dirty, tawdry secrets. The awful choices she'd made to escape him, as necessary as they were unforgivable.

This was no new start. It was a prison sentence. And the only thing she knew for sure was that while Rafael was responsible for her son—the single greatest thing in her life and, as far as she could tell, her singular purpose on this earth—Rafael was also the reason she'd had to burn down every bridge and walk away from everything she'd ever loved.

And Arlo was worth that. Arlo was worth anything.

But that didn't mean she had the slightest idea how she would survive proximity to Rafael again now.

"I don't know how to respond to that," she told him, long after the silence between them had grown strained and awkward and possibly revealing, too. That was what made her tell him as much of the truth as she could. "I don't feel like Lily Holloway. I don't know who that is. I certainly don't understand who she was to you."

"Never fear," Rafael said, his voice soft but somehow containing all the might of those mountains looming up above them, solid rock and sheer, dizzying magnitude, and all of that dark heat besides. "I'll teach you."

Rafael had no idea what to do with himself now that he'd brought Lily and her son—*his* son—back to Italy.

It was a novel, distinctly unpleasant sensation.

He heard his brother walk into the cozy, private study he used as his office in the great old house, but he didn't turn away from the window where he stood. He'd been there some time, still gripped in the same tight fist that had held him fast since Virginia. Before him, the pristine alpine lake stretched off into the low afternoon mists that concealed the small, picturesque village that adorned its far end and the tall mountains that thrust up like a fortress behind it, as if to protect it.

And much closer, down in the gardens that were little more than a suggestion beneath packed and frozen earth this time of year, the five-year-old child who was indisputably his own ran in loopy circles around the woman who claimed she could not remember Rafael at all.

He was certain she could. More than certain. He'd seen it in those lovely eyes of hers the way he'd always seen her need. Her surrender. He knew she was lying as sure as he'd known who she was when he'd seen her on the street.

What Rafael didn't know was *why*.

"Are you planning to speak?" he asked Luca with perhaps more aggression than necessary. "Or will you loom there like one of the mountains, silent and disapproving?"

"I can speak, if you like," Luca replied, sounding wholly unaffected by Rafael's tone, much as he always did. "But the stories I have to tell are far less interesting than yours, I think."

Rafael turned then and eyed his little brother. "I thought you were heading down to Rome tonight."

"I am. I imagine you and Lily have a bit more to talk about than she and I do." The sound of a child's excited laughter wafted up from the gardens then, as if on cue, and hung there between them. Luca only smiled. "All of those interesting stories, for example, that you still haven't seen fit to tell me."

They looked at each other across the relatively small room. The fire licked at the grate. The December wind shook the windows, sweeping down from the heights of the mountains and off the surface of the freezing lake. And outside, a little boy was running hard enough to make himself dizzy in the very same spot they'd done so themselves, though in their case, it had been entirely without any parental supervision from the increasingly unwell woman who had never wanted to be a mother in the first place.

Rafael had never intended to have a child of his own. He didn't have the slightest idea what to do now it turned out he had one, without his permission. Without his knowledge, even. Thanks to a woman who had run from him and then concealed that child's very existence from him for all these years.

Deliberately. She had done this *deliberately*.

He didn't know what he felt. Or more precisely, which dark thing he should feel *first*.

"Have you come to ask me something?" Rafael asked after a moment or two dragged by. "Or is this the sort of tactic you use in negotiations, hoping the other party will fall to pieces in the silence?"

Luca laughed, but he didn't deny that. "I would ask you to confirm that you did, in fact, sleep with our sister—"

"Stepsister," Rafael growled. "A crucial distinction, I think you are aware."

"—but that would be for dramatic effect, nothing more." Luca waved a languid hand. "I already know the answer. Unless you have a contorted tale of a petri dish and a turkey baster you'd like to tell me, in which case, I am all ears."

Luca proceeded to drape himself over the nearest chair, lounging there as if this really was a bit of mildly entertaining theater and not Rafael's life. But then, he supposed that for Luca, it was.

Rafael sighed. "Was there a question in there somewhere?"

"Is this why she ran away, then?" Luca's voice was light. Almost carefree, but Rafael didn't quite believe it. He'd seen the shock on Luca's face when she'd walked into that café.

"I couldn't say why she ran away," Rafael replied evenly. Or faked her own death, if he was to call this situation what it truly was. That was what she'd done, after all. Why pretty it up? "And she doesn't appear to have any intention of telling me."

Luca watched him for a moment, as if weighing his words. "It's uncanny, how much that little boy looks like you. Father might well have a heart attack when he sees him. Or lapse further into dementia, never to return, mumbling on about ghosts in the family wing."

"I will be certain to schedule time to worry about that," Rafael assured him, his lips twitching despite himself. "But as I do not expect the old man and his brand-new child bride until much nearer Christmas, I think we can hold off on the family melodrama until then."

"*Buon Natale*, brother," Luca murmured, and then laughed again. "It will be the most joyous Christmas yet, I'm sure. Ghosts and resurrections and a surprise grandson, too. It's nearly biblical."

"I'm glad you find this amusing."

"I wouldn't say this is amusing, exactly," Luca said then, the laughter disappearing. "But what would be the point in beating you up any further? You've been rolling around in the proverbial hair shirt for the last five years and have taken all the pleasure out of needling you, to be honest."

"There was no hair shirt," Rafael said, trying to keep his tone even, because the penance he'd done for a woman who hadn't actually died was not his brother's business. "It was time to grow up. I did."

"Rafael." Luca shifted in his chair, then blew out a breath, shoving back that unruly hair of his. "You were a wreck when you thought she was dead, and for a long time after. Maybe you should take heart that she is not. All the rest is noise that will sort itself out, surely."

Rafael frowned at him. "Of course I'm pleased that she's not dead, Luca."

"But are you happy she's alive?" Luca asked, with that uncanny insight of his that suggested he was something more than the lazy creature he'd spent most of his life pretending he was. At least in public. "It's not quite the same thing, is it?"

"Of course." But Rafael had waited a moment too long to respond, and he knew it. "Of course I'm happy she's alive. What a thing to ask."

His younger brother studied him for a moment. "Is it that she can't remember you?" His mouth curved slightly. "Or anything else, for that matter?"

"I don't believe that she has forgotten a thing," Rafael said quietly, and it took him a moment to recognize the sheer savagery in his voice, to hear the way it sliced through the air between them, harsh and unmistakable. "Not one single thing. She left."

He did not say, *she left me*, and yet that sat there for a moment in the middle of the room as well. Right there in the center of the priceless rug that was older than the two of them and Lily combined. Obvious and terrible, and Rafael thought he couldn't possibly loathe himself more than he did at that moment.

Luca shifted in his chair, his whole body suddenly gripped with a different kind of tension.

"Rafael," he began. "*Mio fratello*—"

"I'm finished discussing this," Rafael gritted out.

"But I am not." Luca shook his head. "This is not the same. Lily is not our mother. There is no comparison between an accident and what happened here."

"You don't actually know that," Rafael said quietly. Too quietly. It revealed too much and even if he hadn't heard that in his own voice as it hung there between them, he saw it in his brother's eyes.

"Raf—"

"No more," Rafael said, cutting his brother off. "Lily and I will come to terms with what she's actually forgotten and what she's found convenient to pretend she's forgotten, I'm sure. That's quite enough ancient history to dredge up. There's no need to drag our mother into this."

For a moment he thought Luca would protest that. He felt himself tense, as if he thought he might fight back if his brother dared—

You need to pull yourself together, he ordered himself. *This is Luca. He's the only person you love who's never betrayed you.*

"Do you have any particular reason to think she's pretending?" Luca asked after a moment, his voice as light and easy as if they'd never strayed into the muddy waters of their mother's sad fate. He even smiled again. "Most women, of course, would hold you like the North Star deep within them, knowing you even if they lost themselves.

Such is the Castelli charm. I know this myself, obviously. But Lily always was different."

Rafael forced himself to smile. To play off the darkness pounding through his veins even then, whispering things he didn't want to hear.

"She was that."

"Her memory will return or it won't," Luca said carefully, watching Rafael much too closely. "And in the meantime, there is the child. My nephew."

"My son," Rafael agreed.

He didn't think he'd said that out loud before. *My son.* He wasn't prepared for that rush inside, that simmering, inarticulate joy, beating back the darkness. He hardly knew what to make of it.

"Indeed." Luca's dark eyes gleamed. "So perhaps what she remembers, or what happened in this ancient history of yours, is unimportant next to that. Or should be."

"Goodbye, Luca," Rafael said softly, and he didn't care what his brother could read in his tone. He didn't care what he revealed, as long as this uncomfortable conversation ended immediately. As long as Luca left him here to fight his way toward his equilibrium again. Rafael was sure it had to be in there somewhere. "I don't expect to see you again until Christmas. What a shame. You'll be missed. By someone, I'm sure."

"Liar," said his irrepressible brother, wholly unconcerned by his dismissal. "You miss me already."

Rafael shook his head, then turned back to the window and ignored the sound of his brother's laughter behind him as Luca took his leave.

Outside, the little boy—*his* little boy—was still running, the hood of his bright blue coat tossed back and his head tipped toward the sky.

Arlo was a miracle. Arlo was impossible. Arlo was a

perfect, wonderful mistake Rafael hadn't known he'd made, and Rafael already thought he was a pure delight.

But he changed nothing.

He only made Rafael's course of action that much more clear.

The ancient Castelli mansion bristled with the kind of supernaturally perfect staff that Lily had forgotten about over the course of these past five years. Impeccably trained, they made her feel as if *she* was gleaming and perfectly presentable at all times. When in fact it was their ability to clean rooms while she was still in them, produce a phalanx of nannies with credentials in hand to watch Arlo whenever she needed a moment and maintain the elegance all around her so expertly that made it feel quite natural that she should find herself living in it again.

It had been different going in the other direction, from these nonchalant everyday luxuries to the challenges of real life without them, but at the time, Lily had viewed all of that as her penance. And her test. If she could manage it, she'd told herself as she'd waited tables in places the old Lily wouldn't have dared enter, she'd earn the right to raise her child herself.

She'd given herself a deadline. If, by her eighth month of pregnancy, she couldn't come up with a better life than the hand-to-mouth, on-the-run existence she'd fashioned for herself, then she would have to tell Rafael about the baby. Or arrange for him to get custody without directly confronting him, maybe. *Something.* No child deserved to struggle along in poverty at all, but certainly not when his mother could make one phone call and whisk him away from a truck stop diner to a place like this. Lily might have left her life the way she had for what had felt like very good reasons, despite the pain she knew she'd caused—but she hoped she wasn't *that* selfish.

Lily had been six months pregnant when Pepper had walked into her diner, headed home after delivering a pair of rescue dogs from a high-kill shelter in Virginia to their loving new home in Missouri. Maybe it wasn't surprising that they'd hit it off instantly—after all, Pepper had a way with strays.

And when she'd hit that eight-month deadline, Lily had been living in the guest cottage on Pepper's land, with a job she quite enjoyed to go along with it. She'd liked her life there and had seen no reason her baby wouldn't, too. Pepper had felt like the long-lost older sister Lily had never had. And then she'd been more like a doting grandmother to Arlo.

Lily didn't regret a single minute of her time in Virginia, and she told herself she didn't regret keeping Arlo's existence from Rafael, either.

But it was shockingly easy to adjust to life in all of that Castelli luxury again, she found, regrets or no. From the stately ballrooms to the gracious salons to the many libraries, large and small, that dotted the rambling old house, every inch of the place was a song of praise to the ancient Castelli name and a celebration of their many centuries of wealth and prominence. She'd made her way to her favorite library tonight, a week after they'd arrived in Italy, while the nannies she'd have said she didn't need tended to Arlo's nightly bath.

This was what they'd been hired to do, she'd been informed the first night they'd come to spirit him away. Which meant Rafael had decreed it—and in this great house, what Rafael decreed was law. That took some getting used to.

"You always loved this room."

Lily jumped at the sound of his voice. It was as if she'd summoned him out of thin air with a single thought, and it took everything she had not to whirl around and face him, the way a guilty person who remembered exactly how much she'd loved this room might do.

"I do like libraries," she said, trying to sound vague. "Doesn't everyone?"

"You like this one because you said it felt like a tree house," Rafael said, and it was only when she heard how calm and even his voice was that she realized she'd been much too close to snapping at him.

Lily heard him move farther into the cozy room, all dark woods and packed bookshelves and the bay window that sat out amid the leafy green treetops in summer. This time of year the bare branches scratched at the glass and made her think about all the ghosts that stood in this room with them, none of whom she wanted to contend with just then.

She turned to find Rafael much closer than she'd expected. He stood there in casual trousers and a sleek sweater that made her palms itch to touch it—*him*—and she told herself the way her heart leaped inside her chest was anxiety. Panic at this awful role she had to play, when she'd never been any good at pretending much of anything.

But the heat that washed over her told a much different story, especially as it settled low and deep and heavy in her belly. And then began to pulse.

It was then that she realized that she hadn't been alone with Rafael since that cold street back in Charlottesville. Not truly alone. Not like this—closed off in a faraway room in a rambling old house where no one could hear them and no one was likely to intervene even if they could.

Lily's heart began to drum against her ribs, so loud that for a moment she was genuinely afraid he could hear it.

"A tree house?" she asked now. She frowned at him,

then out the window and into the darkness, where the December trees were skeletal at best. Someone who had never been here before would certainly not make the summertime connection. It required having whiled away hours in the window seat, surrounded by all of those leaves. "I don't get it."

His dark gaze was intent on hers, as if he was parsing it—*her*—for lies, though he still stood a few feet away, his hands thrust in his pockets. She supposed that was meant to be a safe distance. But this was Rafael. Nothing about him was safe and there was no distance in the world that cut off that electricity that bloomed in the air between them. Even now, as if nothing had happened. As if it was five years ago and no time had passed.

No car accidents. No Arlo. Just this *thing* that had stalked them both for years.

"How have you enjoyed your week here?" Rafael asked. So mildly, as if he had nothing on his mind save the duties of a host and this was a mere holiday for the both of them.

Lily didn't believe that tone of voice at all.

"It's very pretty here," she said, the way a first-time guest might have. "If a bit bleak this time of year. And obviously, the house itself is amazing. But that doesn't make it feel like any less of a prison."

"You are not in prison, Lily."

"That's not—" She cut herself off. "I don't like it when you call me that."

"I can't call you anything else," he said, a dark fire in his voice, his eyes, and it stirred up that dangerous matching blaze inside her. "It sits on my tongue like lead."

She didn't really want to think about his tongue. "If this isn't a prison, when can I leave?"

"Don't."

"I don't know you. I don't know this place. The fact that

you remember this life you think I had doesn't change the fact that *I* don't remember living it. A blood test doesn't change how I feel."

She thought if she kept saying that, over and over again, it might make it true.

"I'm sorry you feel that way," Rafael said, in a remarkably calm tone that was completely at odds with that harsh look on his dark, beautiful face. "But things are complicated. I can't simply let you go and hope you'll be kind enough to stay in touch. You are somewhat more than a mere flight risk."

Lily thought better of showing him her reaction to that. She might not have been truly alone with him since they'd arrived here, but she'd certainly suffered through too many of these sorts of seemingly innocuous barbs that she worried were actually tests. At the various meals they'd taken together with Arlo, because, she'd been informed, hiding away with a tray in her room was not allowed. Every time Rafael encountered her, in fact.

Was she responding as Lily? Or as someone who didn't know who Lily was? Having to worry over every single word she said or expression she let show on her face was like talking through a stone wall, and she was beginning to feel the weight of it inside her, dragging her down.

"And why not?" she asked crisply. "When you know that's what I want?"

"Because," he said softly, "I am a father."

"Arlo doesn't know you from a can of paint," she snapped at him.

"And whose fault is that?"

The silky rejoinder stopped her short. She could feel her temper pounding in her temples, her throat, down in her gut, goading her on. When she knew the very last thing she could be around Rafael was out of control in any way.

Temper would take her down as fast as passion. Faster. At least if she was kissing him, she couldn't run her mouth at the same time.

Lily blinked. Where had *that* come from?

But of course, she knew. She was in a small room, alone with Rafael. Five years ago he would already have been inside her. There would have been no hesitation, no hands thrust into his pockets and that wary distance. He'd once hitched her up on the back of the deep leather sofa to her right and had her biting her own hand within seconds of closing the door behind them.

She went and sat on that same sofa now and saw a gleam of something edgy and very male in his gaze as she did, telling her he was remembering the same thing. She toed off the short boots she wore, pulled her legs in their warm leggings beneath her where she sat and wrapped her arms around her middle and the oversize tunic of a sweater she wore, with the great big cowl neck that was perfect for drafty old European halls like this one.

"So, tell me your theories," she said, with a calm she didn't feel at all.

Rafael stood where she'd left him, over near the wall of books. He didn't cross over and sit down in the chair across from her. He only studied her.

Looking for weaknesses, she thought, and tried to steel herself.

Because she was well aware that Rafael didn't buy her amnesia story for an instant.

"What theory would you prefer to hear?" he asked after a moment. "I have so many."

This angle, staring up at him from below, was unsettling. It was impossible not to be entirely too aware of every hard plane of his perfect chest, or that ridged abdomen of his. It was hard not to lose herself in the stark male lines of his fine, athletic form, much less that ruthlessness he'd always exuded. But where it had been purely sexual five years ago, now it was tempered. Steelier. Harder. More focused and intent. It made him that much more devastating.

And Lily had to find a way to ignore it. All of it. When she'd never managed to do so before.

You're an addict like any other, she told herself now. Like her mother. Hadn't she sat in those meetings from time to time in those first days on the run, pretending it had been something else that had overtaken and ruined her life so totally? *You know how to do this. One excruciating moment at a time.*

Though heroin didn't talk back, she imagined.

"What do you think happened to me?" she asked him then. "If I'm this Lily person, why do I think I'm someone else?"

His dark eyes glittered, and she knew he was biting back the urge to tell her there was no *if* about it. That she was Lily Holloway, whether she liked it or not. She could practically hear him say it—but to his credit, he didn't.

"What did you think when I asked you about your tattoo in that café?" he asked instead. "Didn't you think it was odd that a total stranger could describe it so perfectly when, according to you, we'd never met before?"

"Of course I did. But I thought everything about you was odd."

"That was it? It didn't cross your mind that what I was saying might be true?"

"Not at all." She eyed him, hoping the tension in her arms as she hugged her legs closer into her chest wasn't obvious. "If I walked up to you and said, oh, hello, your name is actually Eugene Marigold and I know you from our days in Wisconsin, would you believe me?"

His eyes gleamed with a hint of golden amusement that danced down the length of her spine, making her shiver deep within. "It would depend on the evidence."

She shrugged. "I'm here to tell you that the evidence doesn't help. I guess I thought you must have seen my tattoo before."

"You often parade around with it showing, do you?"

Lily stilled. She knew that tone. Possessive. And darkly thrilling to her in a way that felt physical, when she knew she should have found it appalling. *The only appalling thing here is you*, she snapped at herself.

"I wear a bathing suit at the lake sometimes, if that's what you mean by 'parading around.'"

"A rather skimpy bathing costume."

"In America we call them bikinis."

He made a sound that wasn't quite a laugh and then he moved toward her, which made her throat go dry in an instant and every part of her body go stiff—but he only dropped down in the chair across from her.

And that suddenly, Lily was tossed back in time. It was the way he lounged there, so surpassingly indolent, as if nothing on earth could ever truly bother him. She remembered that too well. This was the Rafael she'd known. Provocative. Sensual. Even now, with that considering sort of gleam in his gaze that told her he wasn't the least bit relaxed no matter how he happened to be stretched out in that chair, her body reacted to the memory.

More than simply *reacted*. She burst into long, hot, blistering flames. They shuddered through her, one lick after the next, making her want to writhe where she sat. But she didn't dare move. She hardly dared breathe. And she had to hope against hope he thought she was blushing about the mention of bikinis. Or from the crackling fire in the nearby grate. Who was she kidding? He knew exactly why she'd flushed red, and she knew he did, too.

But none of this was about what Rafael knew. It was about what he could prove.

"How did you come up with the name Alison Herbert in the first place?" he asked, much too quietly, after another heavy moment dragged by, leaving furrows of stone deep in her gut. "You had a very specific biography at the ready. Where did it come from?"

Where indeed, Lily thought darkly. The truth—that she'd bought that driver's license off a girl she'd vaguely resembled in a truck stop parking lot with a week's worth of tips, and had helped herself to that same girl's hastily told life story, too—was obviously out of the question. And she had to bite her tongue against the urge to over-explain and overcomplicate, because that could only make this harder.

She shrugged. "I don't really know."

"I think you can do better than that." A crook of his sensual lips when she frowned at him. He propped up his head against the fingers of one hand like some emperor of old and didn't shift his hard gaze from hers for a moment. "Do you remember your childhood as this Alison?"

She'd had a little more than a week to prepare for this particular performance, and had thought of little else in that time. So she scowled at him now, bristling a bit where she sat.

"Of course." He waited when she paused. She made herself breathe in, then out. Count to ten. "I mean… I think I do."

"Ah."

Lily didn't understand how he could steal all the air from the room when she was looking straight at him and could see with her own eyes that he hadn't moved at all.

She frowned harder in his direction, though it didn't seem to help. If anything, she found it harder to breathe.

"I don't see the point in talking about this," she said then. She jerked her gaze away from his, sure he could read entirely too much on her face, and scowled down at the cuff of her sweater as if it contained the answers to these mysteries. She picked at it with her other hand. "Obviously, what I remember or don't remember is irrelevant. You have the blood work."

"I do."

"And that's why we're here." Lily swallowed, then lifted her head again to meet his gaze. This time, she held it. "But what about you?"

"Me?" He looked faintly amused, or as amused as anyone could look with so much thunder in his gaze. "I know exactly who I am."

"But you were my stepbrother," Lily said, and tilted her head slightly to one side, hoping she looked curious rather than challenging. "How did any of this happen?"

She looked fragile and something like otherworldly tonight, Rafael thought, with her thick strawberry blond hair piled high on her head. It only called attention to the delicate elegance of her fine neck, something he realized he hadn't paid enough attention to five years ago. Here, now, he couldn't think of anything else. She was swallowed up in that oversize sweater, which he imagined was the point of it. The bigger and baggier the sweater, the less of her he could see.

He doubted she realized that without the distraction of that lithe, intoxicating body of hers that still drove him mad, he had nothing to do but parse every single expression that crossed her face and every last telling look in her lovely eyes.

Rafael didn't believe for one moment that she couldn't remember him.

And if she didn't remember him as she claimed, then she couldn't remember what had actually happened between them, and he could paint it any way he liked. If she could remember him, well, it was up to her to interrupt and set the record straight, wasn't it?

After all, this was the woman who had failed to tell him he was a father, that he had a son, *for five years*—and had certainly not come clean about it on her own. If he hadn't seen her on that street in Virginia, would she ever have told him about Arlo? He doubted it. He would never have known.

He almost wished she really did have amnesia. For her sake.

Rafael smiled at her then and felt rather more like a wolf than was wise.

"It's really a very sweet story," he said. He was sure he saw her stiffen. "You were an awkward sort of teenager when our parents got together, ungainly and shy. You hardly spoke."

"What?" She coughed when he looked at her, and she managed to look so guileless that he almost doubted that he'd heard that sharpness in her voice then. Almost. "I'm sorry. Did you say *ungainly*?"

"Many teenage girls have those rough patches," he said, as if he was trying to be comforting. "But I think being around Luca and me helped you a bit. Smoothed out the edges."

"Because you were both such excellent brothers to me?" she asked, and wrinkled her nose in that way he'd always liked a little too much. He still did. "That pushes us straight into icky territory, doesn't it?"

Rafael laughed. "Nothing could be farther from the

truth. We more or less ignored you." He waved a languid hand in the air. "Our father is always marrying various women, the more broken the better, and sometimes they come with children we're expected to treat as family for a while. We all know it's temporary. A form of charity, really." He smiled at her, and there was a bit more color on those remarkable cheeks of hers than there had been before. Though that could also have been the cheerful fire that crackled away beside them. "No, I mean that Luca and I dated a wide selection of very elegant, fashionable, socially adept women. You idolized them, of course. It must have been a master class for a girl like you, from such different circumstances."

She returned her attention to the sleeve of her sweater and fiddled with her cuff. "Were our circumstances so different?"

"I'm really talking more about a certain polish that some girls have. They're born with it, I think." He eyed the growing flush on her cheeks, certain it was her temper and not the fire this time, and kept going. "I hope my honesty doesn't upset you. If it helps, I think European women are better at achieving this polish than American women. Perhaps it's cultural."

"How lucky that I had all of the many women you dated to help me overcome my Americanness," she said evenly. He hoped she was remembering the women he'd dated back then, all of them about as polished as mud, and that her even tone was painful for her. But she only flicked a look at him, her blue gaze unreadable. "Is that what happened? These paragons of womanhood made me one of them and you found you had to date me, too?"

He actually grinned at that and saw the reaction in her clear blue eyes before she dropped them again. But the heat he'd seen there licked over him like wildfire, and his voice was huskier than it had been when he continued.

"You wrote me daily poems, confessing your girlish feelings to me. It was adorable."

"Poems," she echoed flatly. "I find that…amazing. Truly. Since I haven't written a word in as long as I can remember."

"We haven't established how long that is, have we?"

"And how long did I attempt to woo you with teenage poetry?" she asked, with a smile that didn't quite reach her eyes. "You must have found the whole thing embarrassing."

"Very," he agreed. "You were so bad at it, you see."

"Were it not for the existence of Arlo, I'd think this story was heading in a very different direction," she said dryly.

"On your eighteenth birthday," he said, as if recalling a favorite old story instead of making it up on the spot, "you stood before me in a white dress, like a wedding gown, and asked me if I would grant you one wish."

"Oh," she breathed. "Like a fairy tale. Did you say I was eighteen or eight?"

"Eighteen." His voice was reproving, and it was hard to keep himself from laughing. "You were quite sheltered, Lily."

"But not by you, because then the fact that we actually did get together would surely be gross." She smiled faintly at him. "I'm guessing."

"You were sheltered by the strict convent school you attended," he lied happily. She'd been nowhere near a convent in all her life, to his recollection. "You entertained some notion of becoming a nun."

He could almost hear the crackle of her temper, like water against hot metal, though she only swallowed. Hard.

"A nun," she repeated, her gaze narrow on his. "I wanted to become a nun."

He smiled with entirely too much satisfaction. "It was cute."

"And yet somehow we produced a child," she prompted him, a touch of acid in her voice, though her expression was impressively impassive. "Despite the fact I was, apparently, an eight-year-old wannabe nun with no greater ambition than to live in a fairy tale. A poetic fairy tale."

"On your eighteenth birthday you asked me for a kiss," he told her, sitting back farther in his chair and enjoying himself. He couldn't remember the last time in the past five years he'd enjoyed himself quite so much, in fact. "'Please, Rafael,' you begged. 'I want to know what it is to be a woman.'"

"Oh, come on. No one says things like that. Not in real life."

He shrugged. "And yet, you did. Or do you remember it differently?"

"I don't remember it at all," she murmured, and he saw that mutinous light in her eyes. His stubborn girl. "Though that sounds a little bit dramatic, if I'm being honest."

"You were a very theatrical teenager, Lily. The despair of your mother and a trial to all your teachers, or so I was told at the time."

She rubbed her hands over her face. "And yet somehow all this drama led to a secret relationship? That strains belief, doesn't it?"

"That was your call," he told her without a single qualm, watching her for a reaction to what might have been the biggest lie of all, but she only stared back at him. "You begged for a kiss, which, of course, I refused."

"I can't say I blame you. I'd question the man who looked at a gawky teenager in a makeshift bridal gown who'd seriously considered taking up the veil and thought, *I want some of that.*"

Rafael had no idea how he kept from laughing. "I told you that I couldn't possibly kiss such an innocent. That you would have to prove yourself a woman if you wanted me to kiss you like one."

"You felt this was the right approach to an obviously confused teenager?" Lily sniffed. "I wonder if a kind word or two might have been a little more helpful. Or the number of a good therapist."

"I thought you would run screaming back into your sheltered little world." He didn't know when he'd slipped from his fantastical story into something a lot like the truth, but he knew he didn't like it. Rafael stretched out his legs before him and eyed her across the accent rug, where she'd once slipped to her knees and taken him in her mouth while his father and her mother had talked loudly in the hallway on the other side of the door. He remembered the heat of her mouth, the sweep of her tongue, as if it had happened yesterday. So did the hardest part of him. "I thought you were all bark and no bite."

"Let me guess," she said softly. "I bit."

"In a manner of speaking." Rafael remembered that kiss on New Year's Eve. He remembered the taste of her flooding him, and the weight of her thick, wild hair against his palms. He remembered the press of her breasts against his chest and the silky-smooth expanse of the sweet skin at the tops of her thighs, where he shouldn't have reached in the first place. "You decided you needed to prove yourself a woman."

"Was there a series of tests?" Lily asked in that same soft voice, yet with something far edgier beneath it. "A gauntlet of fire, one can only hope?"

"Do you really want the details?"

Her gaze was too hot when it met his. She looked away—but it took a moment. "No."

"You insisted we keep it a secret. You demanded I date other women in public so no one would know. You were determined."

"And you, of course, acquiesced."

"Of course. I am nothing if not a gentleman."

There was a long silence, then. There was only the sound of the fire. The far-off noises that all old houses made, the shift and creak of settling. The moody December weather on the other side of the old glass windows.

His own heart, beating a little too hard for a simple conversation like this one.

"Can I be honest with you?" she asked.

"Always."

"I don't think I believe you."

Rafael couldn't keep from smiling then, and stopped trying. "Do you remember another version of events, then?"

"Of course I don't. You know I don't."

He watched her ball her hands into fists, and took that as a victory. "Then my version will have to stand, as told."

"Let's say that all of this is true." She studied him. "Why would you fall in love with me? The person you describe is a disaster at best."

"Love makes us all fools, Lily," he said quietly.

"You as much as admitted you made all of that up," she pointed out. "Or you wouldn't ask me for a different version."

"Tell me which part," he dared her.

She sat up then, so abruptly it made him blink. She stamped her feet back into her boots, one after the next with a certain nearly leashed violence, and then stood up in a rush. Rafael wanted nothing more than to do the same—but stayed where he was, lounging there as if he'd never in his life been more at his ease.

"This is crazy," she muttered, as much to herself as to

him. But then her blue eyes slammed into his. "What kind of person are you, to play games like this?"

"Do you really want to know the truth?" he asked her, and he wasn't at all languid any longer. He couldn't even pretend. He sat up, never shifting his hard gaze from hers.

"I thought that was the point of you bringing me here. All the truth, all the time. Whether I like it or not."

"Because you knew the truth once, Lily," he said, with a harshness that surprised him even as he spoke. He couldn't seem to contain it. "You lived it. And then you sent your car over the side of a cliff and walked away from it. You had a baby, changed your name and hid in a place no one you'd known before would ever think to look for you. Maybe you don't want to know the truth."

Lily shook her head, more as if she was shaking this off than negating what he'd said, and he viewed that as a victory, too.

"Or," he said in the same tone, with that same edge, "you already know the truth and all of this is a game you're playing for reasons of your own. What kind of person would that make you?"

She stiffened as if he'd slapped her.

"I think you're not right in the head," she threw at him as she started for the door. "Why would you tell me a bunch of lies? How could fake stories of a made-up past do anything but make things worse?"

"I wouldn't worry about it," Rafael replied, and even he could hear the danger in his voice. The menace. And it took everything he had to stay where he was. To let her go when that was the last thing he wanted, ever again. "Chances are, you'll forget that, too."

CHAPTER FIVE

THE HISTORIC CASTELLI palazzo was small by Venetian standards, set on the stately Grand Canal in the shadow of far loftier residences once inhabited by the great and noble families of old Venice. But no matter how many times Lily told herself that, no matter how she reminded herself of the offhanded way her former stepfather had referred to this place as *a pile of sentiment and rising tides* as if it was beyond him why anyone would come here, her first sight of it from the water of the Grand Canal made her breath catch in her throat.

Catch, then hold too tight, as if that much beauty in one place might damage her heart within her chest.

She told herself it was the view. The rise of the old stone building from the depths of the canal as if it was floating there, the quality of the pure gold light that beamed out from within and spilled across the water, like a dark dream made real on this cold, breezy evening. It was the view, she assured herself, not the man who stood so tall and brooding and forbiddingly silent beside her in the private water taxi, as if the wind that ruffled at her hair and made her wrap herself even more tightly in her winter coat was yet one more detail that was far beneath his notice.

He looked like a dark prince, she thought then, as if she was channeling the teenaged poet she'd never been. Made of shifting shadows and the graceful lights that moved over the water like songs. He looked otherworldly. More fable than man.

You need to get a grip, she told herself sternly. *Lose control with this man and you lose everything.*

"It is beautiful, is it not?" Rafael's voice was silky, like the falling night in this nearly submerged city of echoes and arches, mysteries and dreams, and there was no reason at all that it should shiver down the length of Lily's spine like that, then pool too hot at its base. "And not yet sunk into the sea."

"It's lovely, of course, as I'm sure you're well aware," she replied, sounding stiff and unfriendly to her own ears. "I'm sure every guidebook printed in the last three hundred years agrees. But I still don't understand why we're here."

"I told you." He shifted his position against the polished hull of the small, sleek boat that cut through the water as efficiently as he seemed to slice deep into her with that dark look he kept trained on her. Lily wished she'd sat down in the sheltered interior, away from him. But she'd wanted to see Venice more than she'd wanted to avoid him, and contending with Rafael was the price of that decision. "It is the Christmas season. I must make my annual appearance at our neighbors' ball or the world as we know it will come to a shuddering halt. My ancestors will rise from their graves in protest and the Castelli name will ring in infamy throughout the ages. Or so my father has informed me in a series of theatrical voice mail messages."

Her hands clenched tight deep inside her pockets against a certain warmth that threaded its way through her chest and would be her downfall, she knew it. "I don't see what any of that has to do with me. Or why I had to leave my son with strangers to accompany you on some family errand."

Rafael's hard mouth moved then, into that little crook

that undid her. "Do you not? You are the mother of my child—who could not be happier where he is, with a veritable army of nannies to tend to his every whim, as I think you are well aware. Where else should you be but at my side, for all the world to see and marvel at your resurrection?"

Lily didn't know what scraped at her more—that he'd called her the mother of his child with such matter-of-fact possessiveness it made her head spin, or that he claimed he wanted her with him, as if that was the most natural thing in the world.

When the Rafael she'd known had refused, point-blank, to ever keep her anything but his own dirty secret.

Of course, she wasn't supposed to remember that. And for a taut moment, she let herself imagine what it might have been like if she truly couldn't remember him. If she could take all of this—him—at face value. If she could believe him this time around.

But that way lay nothing but madness. Heartbreak and betrayal. She tried to shake it off.

"When you say, 'for all the world to see,' I hope you don't mean that whole paparazzi thing." She frowned, and shook her head. "I work in a kennel in Virginia. I don't want strangers looking at me."

She couldn't read that dark gleam in his gaze then, or the way his hard, lean jaw moved as if he was biting something back.

"You can wear a mask if you like, even if it is not yet *Carnevale*," he said, after a moment. "Many do, though perhaps not out of the same misplaced sense of modesty you seem to feel. Given that you are but a kennel worker. From Virginia."

Lily looked sharply at him at that too-dry tone, then away, as the boat reached the palazzo's low dock and the driver leaped out to pull the ropes taut and bring the sleek vessel in close so they could disembark. Though it seemed Rafael's voice was the tighter noose, wrapped like a hand around her throat.

"But make no mistake, Lily. I will always know who you are."

His voice was like a touch, and she hated that traitorous part of her that wished it really was. More than wished it—*longed* for him in all those ways she was afraid to admit, even to herself. Afraid that once she did, it would be the emotional equivalent of hurling herself off the side of a cliff for real this time, and then what would become of her? But of course, she already knew. *Maybe you don't want to know the truth*, he'd accused her the other night, and he was right. She really didn't want to know it. Because she'd already seen exactly where it led. She already knew exactly what loving him made her do.

At the very least, the fallout of those feelings had turned her into someone she despised.

"It's a clear day," Rafael had said on a bright morning this past week, walking into the private salon in the family wing of the old house where Lily and Arlo had become accustomed to having their breakfast.

Lily had glanced up and lost her breath for a moment at the unexpected *hit* of him. That rangy body of his that he'd dressed that morning in the kind of deceptively casual clothing she knew only appeared to be simple and straightforward. The stretch of exquisite luxury wools across his perfect chest, the way those trousers clung to the lean muscles in his thighs. He looked like some kind of infinitely powerful adventurer, some modern-day Italian prince, as likely to leap over one of the looming mountains outside as he was to take to the nearest throne—

Maybe, she'd thought then, *all those ridiculous lies he*

told you about your absurd and overdramatic teenaged
behavior weren't so far off the mark.

"Thank you," she'd said, with as little inflection as she
could manage, as if maintaining an even tone could repel
him. As if anything could have. She'd looked past him toward the floor-to-ceiling windows, where she could see
what kind of day it was all by herself, then back. "I appreciate the weather report."

Rafael's mouth had moved in that same curve, not quite
a smirk, that had lit her on fire no matter how she'd tried
to tell herself that was simply the old house's unwieldy
heating, not him at all.

"Your appreciation is overwhelming," he'd murmured,
and she didn't understand how he could make that sound
like sex. How he could make *anything* sound like sex when
he said it in that voice of his.

Arlo, meanwhile, appreciated all things Rafael in a pure
and straightforward way that made Lily's heart squeeze
too tight in her chest. And something like shame form a
thick, oily slick deep in her belly. That morning, Arlo had
tossed his arms above his head and started singing at the
top of his lungs, completely unaware of all those dangerous undercurrents swirling through the room.

Lily had forced a smile when Rafael raised a query-
ing brow at her.

"That is the hello song," she'd told him with as much
dignity as she could muster while sitting next to a five-
year-old who was singing and dancing and wriggling
madly in his seat. "He learned it in his preschool. They
sing it every morning."

"I'm honored," Rafael had said, smiling at his son. A
real smile, she'd noted. One of those pure Rafael smiles
she remembered from before that could have knocked them
straight into spring, it had been so bright.

And Lily had officially hated herself, then. Because the smile he'd used when he'd looked at Arlo had been genuine. It had been beautiful. It was lit with pride and longing and a sweetness she'd have said Rafael Castelli could not—did not—possess. Arlo had catapulted himself off the side of his chair and raced around the table at the sight of it, tossing himself at Rafael's legs to bestow one of his heedless, reckless full-body hugs.

Lily hadn't known whether to smile or cry. Especially when Rafael had looked so stunned for a second. He'd put his hand on his son's head as if it belonged there and then he'd smiled down at the little boy as if Arlo was a burst of pure summer sunshine on such a chilly December morning.

And so she'd ruined it.

"He does that to every man he meets," Lily had heard herself say, ugly and sharp.

The words had hung there in the air of the salon between them. They'd seemed to grow louder with every second, as if they were amplified off the graceful old walls. If she could have reached into the air and plucked them back, thought better of them and kept them to herself, she would have done it.

But there was no repairing the kind of damage she'd always done to this man, and him to her. There was only the living with it.

Rafael's smile had dimmed, then disappeared altogether, and he'd taken his time looking back at her. His gaze had been dark and something much too bleak and furious at once, and it had hurt as much as if he'd thrown something back at her. More, perhaps. Lily kept thinking she couldn't feel any more horrible than she already did, and then sure enough, she found there was a darker, deeper, far worse place.

This is what you do, she'd told herself. *When you're with him, this is who you are.* She'd wanted to say that out loud. To remind him that they'd always ended in the same ugly place—but she couldn't say a word. She'd had to sit and stew in it instead.

"It's clear enough to walk down to the village today," Rafael had said after a long, heavy sort of moment, when she'd thought he could see all the ugliness inside her. When she'd imagined it filled the whole room—the whole sprawling length of the house. Arlo, happily, had seemed completely oblivious, still clinging to his father's legs and chanting something new and bright. "I thought it would be a pleasant family excursion, assuming you're not too busy coming up with further vicious comments to fling at me."

Lily had refused to apologize to him, but still, her throat hurt as if she had more than one apology stacked there. She'd swallowed hard against it. And maybe it would have been different if she hadn't tried to take him out at the knees. Maybe then she might have come up with some way to resist him. But she'd made that glorious smile of his go away because she was a terrible person, and she didn't seem to have any resistance in her just then.

And he'd used the word *family*.

"That sounds lovely," she'd said, her voice hoarse with all the things she couldn't say. The things she didn't want to admit she could feel. The memories she'd been terribly afraid he could see all over her face. "Thank you."

Lily jolted back into the present to find Rafael studying her expression in that way of his that made her forget to breathe. She kept herself from scowling her reaction at him by sheer force of will, and realized only after a long, shuddering beat of her treacherous heart that he was holding out his hand to her. And waiting for her to take it.

She wanted to touch him about as much as she wanted

to fling herself off the side of the boat into the frigid waters of the Grand Canal and swim for it, but she swallowed that down, aware that he was measuring her reaction. That he was clocking exactly how much time it took her to look from that extended hand back up to his face. That, worse, he could probably read every last thought she had as she did it.

Because she was perfectly aware that he knew she could remember him.

He still couldn't *prove* that she could.

"I only want to help you from the boat, Lily," he said softly, the hint of a dark amusement in his voice.

"That is another lie." She hadn't meant to say that. She should have swallowed that down with all the rest of it, she knew that. And maybe to prove how little he bothered her, to herself if nothing else, she slid her hand into his.

It was a mistake. She'd known it would be.

It didn't matter that they both wore gloves to ward off the cold. It didn't matter that she couldn't feel the slide of his skin against her palm or the true heat of his hand. She could feel his strength. She could feel that leashed power of his like a deep, dark ricochet inside her, flooding her with sensation she didn't want, as dangerous as the mysterious Venetian night all around them.

There was no curve at all to that hard mouth of his, then. Rafael's gaze locked to hers.

Heat. Passion. Need.

It slammed into her. It made her feel distorted. Altered. She moved then, jerky and uncertain, as if the world was as rickety beneath her feet as the boat. As the dock that extended out from the palazzo's first-level loggia. As the grand houses of Venice themselves, arrayed around them up and down the canal on their ancient and uncertain ground—some dark with disuse and age, some lit from within like sets of perfect Christmas ornaments made from local Murano glass—and none of them as safe as they were beautiful.

Just like Rafael.

Lily climbed up onto the dock with more alacrity than grace and then dropped his hand as if he'd burned her.

And he didn't have to laugh at her, though she could sense more than hear the deep, dark rumble of it. It was already inside her, where she was still so attuned to him, a part of him. As if they were still connected that way— deeper than sex, like a fire in the blood nothing had ever been able to quench. Not time, not distance. Not betrayal. Not her own supposed death. She began to understand that nothing ever would. That she'd been kidding herself all these long years, imagining it could ever be otherwise.

The palazzo loomed before her, its graceful upper floors gleaming bright against the dark like some kind of beacon, and Lily assured herself it was nothing more than the cold wind sweeping down the canal from the lagoon in the distance and slapping against her face that made her eyes water.

It's the cold, she assured herself. *It's only the cold.*

But then she felt his hands on her, turning her to face him, and she knew better. She was doomed. They were both doomed. They'd been destined to do nothing but rip each other apart since the moment they'd met and set themselves on this terrible collision course that destroyed them both. Over and over again.

She could see it in that stern set to his beautiful mouth. That bold fire in his gaze. Worse, she could feel it in the way she simply…melted. Everything inside her turned soft and ran sweet, and she thought she'd never wanted anything more in all her life than the press of that mouth of his against hers again.

Just one more time, she told herself, almost wistfully, as she looked up at him.

But she knew that was the biggest lie of all.

"Don't kiss me," she whispered then, too quick and too revealing. "I don't want you to kiss me again."

Rafael's stern mouth was so close then—*so close*—and that look in his eyes was enough to raze whole cities, and there was no disguising the way it made her tremble, too. She didn't try.

"Speaking of lies," he said, and drew closer still, his arms moving around her to hold her there in a parody of a lover's embrace.

Or perhaps it was no parody, after all.

She braced her hands against his chest, though she couldn't have said if she was pushing him away or, far more worrying, simply holding him there. "It's not a lie just because you don't like it."

He studied her for a moment, and Lily forgot where they were. What continent, what year. What city. There was nothing but that dark gold brilliance in his gaze, the riot deep inside her, and her ever more fragile resistance. He shifted, raising one gloved hand to smooth over her cheek, the leather both a caress and a punishment, as it was not the lick of heat his bare skin would have been.

She imagined he knew that, too.

"Relax," he said, and he sounded far too amused, then. As if she was the only one torn asunder by this. The only one so affected. "I'm not going to kiss you here. It's far too cold."

"You mean public."

There was a dangerous gleam in his eyes then. "I mean cold."

"I don't understand what the temperature has to do with it." She sounded far more cross than was wise. Rafael's mouth curved.

"The next time I kiss you, Lily, I won't be as thrown as I was on the street in Virginia. There will be nothing but our usual chemistry." He shrugged, though the hand against her cheek tightened, and she knew then that he wasn't nearly as unaffected as he seemed. "And you know what happens then."

She did. A thousand images surged through her then, one brighter and more sinfully wicked than the next. A messy, slick tumult of his mouth, his hands. The thrust of his body deep into hers. The taste of his skin beneath her tongue, the hard perfection of him beneath her hands. Salt and steel.

The ache, the fire. The impossible, unconquerable fire.

"No," she gritted out, glaring at him no matter how much emotion she feared was right there in her eyes to make a liar of her. "I don't know what happens."

He dragged his thumb over her bottom lip, his mouth cruel and harsh and no less beguiling, because he knew exactly what it did to her. The thick heat that wound tight and dropped low, nearly making her moan. Nearly.

"Then you'll be in for quite a ride." He looked at her as if he was already inside her. Already setting a lazy, mind-wrecking pace. "It's uncontrollable. It always has been."

Lily jerked her head back, out of his grip, much too aware that he let her. That he could have stopped her, if he chose. His hand dropped from her face and she wanted to slap that deeply male, wholly satisfied look straight off his face. She had to grit her teeth to keep from doing it.

"I don't know what that means," she told him, her voice as frigid as the air around them. As the dark, mysterious waters of the canal behind him. "I feel certain I don't *want* to know what it means."

His dark eyes were hooded as they met hers. He still looked like they were already having sex. As if it was a foregone conclusion. As if this was nothing more than foreplay—and every part of her body burst into jubilant flame at the sight.

"It means I kiss you, then I'm inside you," he told her, in a voice straight out of those wild, feverish dreams she lied and told herself were nightmares. She'd been telling herself that for years. "Always."

"I will take that as a threat," she threw at him and stepped back, as if that tiny wedge of space could make what he said less true. His mouth shifted, and she thought she'd never seen him look more like a wolf than he did then.

And she didn't think she'd ever wanted him more.

"You may take it any way you choose," he told her, all dark intent and certainty. "It is a fact, Lily. As inevitable as the dawn after a long, cold night. And as unavoidable."

Rafael thought she might run.

He set footmen at the door to her bedchamber and found himself rather more grim than he should have been as he considered what pointless attempt she might make to escape him this time. Yet despite his dark imaginings as the hours crept by, no alarm was raised.

And when the clock struck the appointed hour, Lily appeared at the top of the grand stair inside the palazzo like every last one of the fantasies he'd conjured up over the past five years.

He'd planned this well, he'd thought. He'd had the gown shipped in from Milan, had dispatched servants to tend to her hair and her cosmetics. He'd thought he'd prepared himself for the inevitable result.

But it was one thing to imagine Lily, *his Lily*, alive and well and dressed like a member of the scrupulously high-

class Venetian society they would mix with tonight. It was
something else to see her again with his own eyes.

Rafael had never been so glad of that long staircase
that swept down from the upper floor of the palazzo to
the main level where he stood.

It gave him time to compose himself. Lily moved like
water, grace and beauty in every light step, as she made
her way toward him. Her honey-colored hair was piled high
on her head, held fast with a series of glittering combs,
just as he'd asked. The dress he'd had crafted to her pre-
cise measurements cupped her gorgeous breasts and then
swept in a wide arc toward the floor, managing to hint at
her lithe figure even as it concealed it in yards upon yards
of a deep, mellow blue-green that made her seem to glow
a pale, festive gold.

He'd never seen anything more beautiful.

And then she stopped at the foot of the stair, this perfect goddess with her heart-shaped and heart-stopping face
that made his own battered heart ache within his chest,
and scowled at him.

"I want a mask," she said.

Rafael blinked. And tried to wrestle his roaring, possessive reaction into some kind of manageable bounds.
It wouldn't do to throw her down on the stairs, to lick his
way into her heat and taste the secrets she still hid from
him. It wouldn't do to rip that perfect gown into shreds
where she stood, the better to worship the curve of her
sweet hip and the lily tattoo that he knew danced there,
out of sight.

"Why?"

He thought he sounded relatively polite and civilized,
all things considered, but her scowl only deepened.

"Do I need a reason? You said people wear them."

"So they do." He couldn't let himself touch her. Not

until he was certain he could keep himself in check. "This is Venice. But I want you to tell me why *you* want one."

Lily tilted up that marvelous chin of hers and he felt it like a bolt of heat lightning, straight into his aching sex. Soon he would be unable to walk entirely, and those stairs would look that much better. He could pull her astride him, taking the cold floor against his back, and he could—

He shook the vivid images away. Somehow.

"I want to pretend to be one of the great Venetian courtesans," she told him sharply, as if she'd read his mind. She eyed him, and Rafael was sure she had. "Isn't that why you brought me here? So I could recreate history?"

"Unless you'd like to recreate our own history right here on the hard marble steps," he said with a quiet savagery, "I suggest you try again."

She looked at him, then away, though that proud chin remained high.

"I don't want to be recognized. I don't particularly enjoy being treated like a ghost from beyond the grave." He watched the elegant line of her lovely neck as she swallowed. "Especially when I can't remember the person they'll think I am."

"I will remember for the both of us."

He didn't know where that pledge came from, as if he was a good man and this was that kind of situation. And then she looked back at him, her blue eyes lit with a kind of warm, wry humor that he thought might be the end of him right there. And she didn't quite smile, but he felt it as if she did. Like a gift.

"That's what I'm afraid of," she said.

And Rafael found he couldn't speak. He summoned the nearest servant with a lift of his finger and was glad of the few moments it took to produce a golden demimask, the perfect foil for her gown. For her lovely face.

She reached out for it, but he anticipated that and ignored her. He stepped closer to her than was entirely wise and fit the mask to her face carefully, something like reverently. He ran his fingers along the edges and smoothed it over the top of her elegant cheekbones, and felt the sweet reward of that catch in her breath and then the shiver of it, just that little bit ragged, against his hands.

"There," he said, and he sounded like a stranger. "Now no one will know who you are but me."

Lily's eyes met his through the mask, and he thought they were troubled. Too dark. Something like lonely.

Or maybe that was him.

"I thought that was the point," she whispered, and her voice was as thick as it was accusing, with that undercurrent of something like grief besides. "I thought that was what you've been at such pains to show me. That no one but you does."

"Or ever will," he agreed, more growl than vow.

And he couldn't do what he wanted to do, not then and there, so he did the next best thing. He took her hand and led her out into the night.

CHAPTER SIX

THEY TOOK A water taxi to the party, which was being held in a stately Renaissance-era palazzo that appeared to genuflect toward the dark waters of the Grand Canal. As they came in toward the dock wreathed in holiday lanterns, Lily tipped her head back to gaze up at three full stories of blazing lights from every finely carved window. Music poured out into the night, folding in on itself against the water and the stone buildings of the city, and elegantly dressed partygoers laughed loud enough to spike the breeze.

And Lily was finding it very, very difficult to breathe. At least she had the mask tonight, she thought. Not only would it conceal her identity from the rest of the world a little while longer, she hoped it might go a long way toward hiding her thoughts from Rafael, too. He read her far too easily.

The thought of what, exactly, he might be reading on her face and in her eyes at any given moment—well. That didn't exactly help her breathe any better. She tried to conceal that, too, as she slipped out of her warm cape and left it in the cabin of the water taxi Rafael had hired for the night, as directed.

Rafael handed her out of the boat when it reached the grand palazzo's guest dock, and Lily was proud of herself when she simply climbed out, as if touching him was nothing to her. Then he took her arm as they walked up the elegant steps toward the festive great hall, its doors flung open to the night as if the cold dared not enter and the dark had best submit to the blaze of so many torches. He was warm beside her, and something like steel, and Lily told herself her awareness of him was a warning, that was all.

Beware. That was what her pulse was trying to tell her as it beat out a frenetic pattern against her neck. *Be careful here. With him.*

Nothing more than a warning.

Inside the open central hall of the magnificent palazzo, it was like a dizzying sort of dream. Like being swept up into a jewel-studded music box and meant to twirl along with all the gorgeous creatures who were already there in all their finery, moving this way and that across the marble floors and beneath the benign majesty of priceless glass chandeliers some two stories above. Rafael excused himself to go and do his duty to their hosts, his neighbors, leaving Lily to find her way to one of the great pillars and stand there, happily anonymous. She braced herself against the stout, cool marble as if it could anchor her to the earth. She didn't know where to look first. A single glance at the scene before her and she felt glutted, over-done on sensation and stimuli.

On this particular Venetian magic.

Lily had certainly attended her share of fancy parties in the past. She'd even gone to a great ball in a Roman villa once, with the entire Castelli family and her own mother in attendance. She'd attended glamorous weddings in stunning locales international and domestic, exclusive charity events that had seemed to compete for the title of Most Over the Top, and had once danced in a brand-new year with most of Manhattan spread out at her feet in a desperately chic four-story penthouse on Central Park West.

But all of that had been a long time ago, and none of it had been Venice.

Tonight, everyone glittered the way the finest diamonds did, unmistakably well cut and intriguingly multifaceted. The women were nothing less than stunning, while each and every man was distractingly debonair. Was it the people or the place itself? Lily couldn't tell. The air itself seemed richer, brighter. There were jovial feathers and the occasional masks, striking black tie and sumptuous couture. Gowns and jewels and sartorial splendor crowded the whole of the expansive first level of the palace, a gracious orchestra played holiday-tinged music from a raised marble dais that seemed to hover as if by magic just above the throng and the sleek marble dance floor in the center of the grand space opened up to the night sky above, yet was surrounded by so many clever little heaters that it was impossible to feel the mid-December chill.

Lily shivered anyway, and she knew it wasn't the temperature. It was the sheer, exultant decadence. This was a sinking city, a nearly forgotten way of life, and yet not a single bright and shining person before her seemed the least bit aware of any of those unpleasant realities as they danced and laughed and pushed back the night.

Something inside her turned over too hard, then ached.

"Come," Rafael said, his mouth against her ear and the steel expanse of his chest at her back, and that ache bloomed instantly into something darker. Thicker. Infinitely more dangerous. "I want to dance."

"There must be hundreds of women here," Lily replied, her eyes on the spectacle before her. It was overwhelming, yes—but he was worse. He was so much worse and infinitely more tempting. "I'm sure one of them would dance with you. If you asked nicely."

His laughter was a dark and silvery thing, light against

her ear and then, deep inside her, a tectonic shift that sent tendrils of need shooting off in all directions, and she couldn't bring herself to jerk away from him the way she knew she should.

"I don't want to dance with them, *cara*. I want to dance with you."

Lily wanted to dance with him in this magical palace more than she could recall wanting anything, ever, which was precisely how she knew she shouldn't do anything of the kind. She pulled her head away from that sweet brush of his mouth against her ear, though it took her much too long and hurt a bit too much to break that connection. When she turned to face him, his gaze was trained on the upper swells of her breasts where they rose above her bodice, where she could feel the goose bumps from his proximity prickling to life. The truth of her reaction to him. Obvious and unmistakable, no matter what she said.

Rafael took a long time raising that dark gold gaze to meet hers, and when he finally did, his expression was a molten, simmering thing that nearly made her moan out loud.

"I don't dance," she told him. Quickly, before she could betray herself by saying nothing at all—by letting him simply sweep her along with him. He stood there, tall and darkly beautiful and wearing black tie as if it had been crafted specifically as an homage to his perfect masculine form, and she wanted to cry. Sob. Scream. Anything to break that rising tension inside her. Anything to break the hold he had on her. Anything but what she felt called to do, down deep in her bones, and in that deep, lush throb between her legs. "I mean, I don't think I know how."

"You do."

"I don't know what good it will do to tell me that, if I can't remember and trip all over your feet and make a terrible scene. I doubt that's the kind of spectacle you want at a party like this."

She only realized how snappish she sounded when he reached over and traced the lower edge of her mask with a single finger. It was pressure, not heat. He wasn't touching her, not really, and there was absolutely no reason whatsoever that her pulse should speed up like that, or her breath should hitch. Noticeably.

More evidence against her, she knew.

"You don't have to remember, Lily," he said, his gaze much too bright and his voice a low, caressing thing that did everything his finger did and more, winding inside her and making her whole body clench tight and hot and needy. "You only need to follow where I lead."

Rafael didn't wait for her answer, which she supposed was some kind of blessing. Or more likely, it being the two of them, a curse. He simply reached down, took her hand and led her out on to the floor.

And Lily told herself she was blending in with the crowd here, nothing more. That she didn't want to be recognized at all tonight, which meant she also didn't want to draw any attention to herself by causing a scene. It was bad enough that Rafael was so gorgeous and so instantly recognizable—she could see heads turn as he cut through the crowd, something that was so commonplace to him, clearly, that he didn't even seem to notice it as it happened. Lily told herself it was the right thing to do, to go along with him so obediently, so easily. That she was simply making sure she remained anonymous and unremarkable— just another well-dressed woman in a demimask, one of many here tonight.

But then he turned and took her in his arms, and Lily stopped thinking about anything but him.

Rafael.

His sensual mouth was a grim line, but she could see that searing intensity in his eyes, and it made her tremble deep inside. She had no defense against that hand that wrapped around hers, or the one that settled low on her back, as if she was naked, as if the sleek fall of her dress was no barrier at all. He could have pressed a burning coal to her bare skin and she thought that might have affected her less. She swallowed hard as she slid her own hand into place, over the taut, corded muscles of his sculpted shoulder, and felt the bright hot heat of him blaze into her as if he was a radiator.

Lily felt scalded. Turned pink and raw from even that much fully clothed contact—but all she could seem to do was stare up at him, her lips parting on a ragged breath, his own dark need like a physical presence she could feel as well as her own.

She knew she should have done something—anything—to lighten the moment, to wrench herself away or to conceal how she shook at his touch, at that predatory, possessive look in his dark eyes, but she didn't.

She didn't do a thing. And for a moment they only stood there, staring at each other. Stock-still as the dance wove and swirled around them, as if they were the center of a carousel, and the only thing Lily knew for that moment—that endless eternity—was that they were touching at last. After five long and lonely years, she was in his arms again.

Where you belong, some suicidal part of her whispered. *Where you have always belonged and always will.*

And then Rafael began to move.

Lily felt as if she was floating. She had no sense of him, of her, as separate entities—there was only the glory of the waltz and of his masterful touch, the way they flew across the floor as if they were all alone, the way his gaze wrecked her and remade her with every step. She forgot where she ended and he began. She was too close to him, her hand gripping his hand and her fingers digging deep into his shoulder, and his palm against her back was a revelation.

Around and around they went. And it was like falling. It was like flying.

It was all the poetry she'd never written, step by well-executed step, pooling in the white-hot space that was barely there between them.

And then the song blended into something else, something far more Christmas inspired than sweepingly romantic. Lily blinked as if a spell had been lifted. Rafael slowed, muttering out what sounded like one of his fanciful Italian curses beneath his breath.

"What's the matter?" she asked, but she was too dazed still to worry overmuch. Besides, she felt *everything*. The press of her fine clothes against her heated skin. The warmth of the great room, of his hard, hot hand in the small of her back, flirting with the upper swell of her bottom. The way he held her against him, his strong thigh too close to that wild, wanton place that hungered for him the most.

She was molten and he was steel and she *wanted*. God help her, how she always *wanted* this man, no matter what.

Rafael didn't respond to her halfhearted question, and Lily didn't care. The look on his face was stark, almost pained, and she exulted in it. Because she knew exactly what it was—what had happened to him in the course of that waltz. It was the same thing that always happened, no matter what they did. It was this *thing* of theirs that had destroyed them so many times already it hardly bore tallying up any longer. But here, now, at a fanciful pageant of a Christmas party in the depths of December in this city of light and magic, she couldn't manage to care about all that the way she knew she should.

It was as if that dance was inside them now, insistent and elegant, elemental and demanding.

He made a sound that was more that wolf in him than the genteel and civilized man he was playing tonight, and Lily felt her nipples go hard against the constriction of her dress's bodice and her toes cramp up in her impractical shoes. Then Rafael was moving again, not dancing this time, but striding through the crowd. Pulling her with him as he went, weaving in and out of the dancing couples and then propelling them down a dimly lit corridor off to the side of the main hall, where ancient oil paintings featured dour and scowling men on the ornately paneled walls while smaller doors led off into the bowels of the palace.

"I don't think this is open to the public," Lily said dubiously, looking around with a frown. "I don't think we're supposed to be back here. Do you?"

"I cannot imagine caring about anything less than that," Rafael muttered. And then something else in gruff Italian. "*Mi appartieni.*"

Or that was what she thought he said, it was so fierce and low. *You belong to me.* And then he swung her around so her back was against the nearest wall. She had a glimmering moment to take in the nearly savage look on his dark face, and then his mouth was on hers.

And all hell broke loose.

This wasn't a moment of shocked surprise on the street. This was nothing but need, pure and greedy and entirely, exultantly mutual.

Lily couldn't pretend otherwise. She didn't bother to try.

This was fire. This was passion. Their history and that electric perfection that charged so hot and bright between them, an instant conflagration. Lily burned. She wrapped herself around him, she forgot herself completely and she let him set them both alight.

Rafael kissed the way he did everything. With sheer, uncompromising ruthlessness and devastating skill. He took over her mouth, tasting her again and again, shoving her back into the wall and using it to keep her exactly where he wanted her. He made a low noise as he kissed her, over and over, as if he couldn't get enough. As if it would never be enough.

As if there was no word for *enough* in either one of their languages.

He held her face between his hands, and he angled his head, blasting the kiss straight into another level of sheer, dizzying sensation. Lily felt her knees go weak and her whole body seem to shake, and still she met every thrust of his tongue, tasting him and taking him in her turn, each kiss as drugging and impossible and wildly delirious as the next.

She must have dreamed the taste of him a thousand times since she'd walked away from that life, from him, but the reality was better. *So much better.*

Rafael shifted, his hands moving from her face to test the shape of her breasts through the smooth fabric of her bodice, and she knew from the appreciative noise he made precisely when he found the stiff peaks. But then it was her turn to cry out when he covered them with his palms and pressed into them, rough and greedy and infinitely knowing, making her throw her head back and arch into his touch for more of that delicious pressure.

He followed her mouth with his, as if he was unwilling to lose her taste for even a moment, and she didn't know which one of them strained toward the other. Who moved, who touched. Who took, who gave. It was all a wild, brilliant tangle of sensation. Need and longing and their age-old ability to drive each other mad, like an explosion that kept going off. And off. Without end.

She had to pull away from that hard, clever mouth of his for a moment to breathe, or at least to try. The hall they stood in was still as dark and deserted as before, but the lights and music beckoned just there, just out of reach through that far-off arch, so many people *right there* who could walk in on them at any moment—

The way it had always been. Desire and the risk of discovery, all knotted together and hidden away where only they could see it, feel it, succumb to it.

And then she forgot about their past, about the party and the people and the whole damned world, because his hands were on her long skirt and then beneath it, and he was urging her leg over his hip with those sure, hard hands, his mouth an open fire against her neck.

Lily didn't think. She burned.

She wrapped her arms around his neck and she gripped him with her leg as he reached between them, and then his gaze found hers. Dark and wild. She felt her mouth drop open. She saw his jaw clench tight as he dealt with his trousers. And then his fingers were moving her panties to one side and the thick, blunt head of his hardness was probing her entrance.

She shook. Everywhere. She shook and she shook and she'd forgotten it, this glorious shaking from the inside out. She'd forgotten how visceral this was, how necessary. Like breath.

Only better.

"I told you," he gritted out. "One kiss. That's all it ever takes."

And then he thrust deep inside her. Hard and deep and true.

Perfect and *Rafael*, after all this time.

Lily fell to pieces, shattering into a thousand fragments at that glorious fit, and only then did he move. Each thrust wilder and deeper than the last. The fever of it, the wild and glorious dance, catching her up when she would have come down and winding her tighter and tighter all over again.

As if all of this need was new.

As if they were.

He slid a hand down to her bottom to lift her against him, pulling her higher until she crossed her legs around him and gripped his shoulders, and then he leaned her back against the wall, braced them with his other hand and hammered himself into her.

Lily loved it. She more than loved it. It was coming home, drenched in fire. It was Rafael. It was *them*.

Again. At last.

And when she threw back her head and came apart again, biting her lip to keep from screaming though her throat ached, he groaned out her name against the side of her neck and followed.

Rafael had no idea how long they stood there like that.

His breath came so hard it almost hurt, he rested his forehead against hers while he tried to catch it and he understood that he had not felt this *rightness* in so long he'd begun to think he'd imagined the whole thing. *Her.* The way they moved together, the sheer and blazing poetry of their lovemaking that had been the only thing he'd thought about some years.

If anything, he'd minimized her effect on him. Her power over him. The beauty of this wild flame that still danced so brightly between them.

He was already hardening again inside her, and he moved his hips experimentally, but it was still the same. That desperate heat. That wildness like a thirst, that all these years later he still had no earthly idea how to quench. He still didn't want to do anything but drown in it. In her.

Lily had never been anything but a revelation to him. That hadn't changed.

But she pushed against him. Then again, harder, and he realized she'd gone stiff in his arms.

"Let me down," she said, her voice thick and something like dangerous, edgy and tight.

Rafael angled himself back, little as that appealed, and then helped her lower her legs to the floor. He bit back a satisfied smile when she sagged slightly, then gripped the wall, as if her knees were precarious beneath her.

But he felt his amusement fade when he met her tormented gaze.

"Lily," he began, reaching over to brush her cheek, not entirely surprised that she was trembling uncontrollably. He could feel it like a series of earthquakes, rippling over her, through her. He felt the same in him. "*Cara*, surely—"

"I can't do this again!" she threw at him. She made a sharp sound as if she was in pain, or as if she hadn't meant to speak. Her eyes were much too dark, and he tucked himself back in his trousers as he studied her expression, as she splayed out a hand over her middle as if she ached while her dress fell back into place all around her as if they'd never touched at all. He found he hated it. "I can't *do* this!"

"Lily," he said again, but it was as if she couldn't hear him. As if there was a storm enveloping her where she stood, only a few inches away from him and yet somewhere else entirely.

"Look where we are!" she hissed at him. She slashed a hand in the direction of the party down the hall, her face contorted and moisture leaking down her cheeks from behind the demimask she still wore. "We might as well have put on a show in the center of the dance floor! Anyone could have seen us!"

He made an impatient noise. "No one did."

"You don't know that. You *hope* that. And it's as child-ish and immature and *irresponsible* now as it was five years ago—except worse, because what happens to Arlo if our sexcapades make the tabloids this time?"

Rafael started to speak, to reassure her again, but then stopped. Froze, more like, into a column of sheer and solid ice where he stood. He felt something like light-headed. As if the great stone palazzo had turned on its end and landed square in the center of his chest.

"What did you say?" He realized he'd asked that in Ital-ian and translated it into clipped English, his pulse like a clanging bell in his temples.

"I can't do this!" she hurled at him, as if he hadn't spoken. "I know exactly where this leads. Me, alone on the side of the road, with no choice but to run away from my entire life. You're heroin and I'm little better than a junkie and everything between us is toxic, Rafael. *It al-ways has been.*"

And then she whirled and threw herself back toward the crowd, not seeming to notice or care that she was still unsteady on her feet. The mad, elegant whirl was still car-rying on just on the far side of the nearest archway, bright and loud, and she lurched toward it as if she might fall over in her haste to escape him—as if she wouldn't much care if she did.

While Rafael stood there in the dim hallway, as stunned as if she'd clubbed him over the head. She might as well have.

She remembered. She knew.

It had been one thing to suspect she remembered. It was another to have her confirm it.

He heard a low, inarticulate noise and understood he'd made it. That it had welled up from deep inside him, from that dark place where he'd locked these things away—

Then, feeling blinded somehow by the intensity of what pounded into him in waves, blinded and yet focused and understanding that was as much the force of his temper as anything else, he went after her.

He caught up to her on the steps of the palazzo, outside near the canal. She whirled around before he could take her elbow, as if she'd heard him coming and had known it was him by the sound of his feet against the stone, and she dashed moisture from her cheeks with her hands clenched in fists.

Rafael told himself he didn't care if she cried. That the very least she could do, after what she'd done to him, was shed a few tears.

It took him long moments to recognize that the moisture on her face was not tears at all. It was snow. It fell all around them, soft and silent, disappearing as it met the water of the canal, the dock at their feet, the lovely bridge lit up in the distance. It was possibly the only thing in the world more beautiful than this treacherous liar in front of him, and he couldn't bring himself to care about that, either.

"You lied." He hardly sounded like himself, and he didn't dare reach for her. He didn't trust himself to touch her just then. She had finally admitted the truth. That she had betrayed him so terribly he could hardly make sense of it, and in that moment he was so hollow and so desperate he didn't know what he might do. For the first time in his life, he didn't know himself at all. "You lied all this time. You hid from me, on purpose. You deliberately kept my son from me for *five years*. Then you lied even more when I found you."

He didn't realize, until he heard the echo of his own voice on the water, that he was not exactly speaking softly. Standing on the steps of a Venice palazzo in the snow with a woman long presumed dead, who had been his stepsister when alive, was not exactly discreet.

But she didn't cower. Lily—and she was wholly Lily, *his* Lily, and she had never been anything else, goddamn her—laughed. There was nothing like joy in it. It was a terrible sound, as wretched as he felt, and he thought it must have hurt her. He hated that he cared about that. That her pain mattered to him when his clearly did not register with her at all.

"Which glass house should we throw stones at tonight, Rafael?" she demanded, her voice as awful as that brittle, broken laugh, as his own had been. "This is what we do. This is who we are and who we've always been. We hurt each other. Again and again and again. What does it matter how?"

"You faked your death!" he roared at her, through the snow and the cold and the echo of the music pouring out from inside the grand palace that rose up behind them in all its Christmas finery. Then he checked himself, though it cost him. "How is anything I did to you equivalent?"

"I didn't fake it." She was breathing so hard it was as if she was running, but she was standing still, just as he was. As if they were both frozen together here in this horrid moment of truth. As if there could be no escaping it, no avoiding it, for either one of them. "I simply didn't come forward and correct anybody when they thought the worst. It's not the same thing."

He didn't recognize the harsh, nearly violent feeling that rushed through him then, nearly taking him from his feet. He took a step back, and the world rushed back at him, reminding him again that they were standing outside, in public, in view of most of Venice and half the world, airing laundry so dirty he thought exposure to it could contaminate the whole of Italy.

He had to contain this. He had to lock this down before it consumed him whole. Before he looked behind the stunned fury that worked in him and truly let himself feel what lurked there on the other side—

But that was for another time. Another place. Rafael whistled for his water taxi, and his driver appeared from the shadows so quickly he couldn't help but wonder how much the man had overheard. He couldn't do anything about that, so he took Lily's arm again instead.

He thought the sheer audacity of her betrayal might have dimmed his raging, timeless, insatiable lust for her—but it was the opposite. The moment he touched her, he hungered for her as if he hadn't just had her. It was almost as if he wanted her *more*, knowing what she'd done to him.

You've never been anything but wildly obsessed where she was concerned, he told himself then. *Why should this surprise you?*

"Not here," he bit out at her, and he didn't let himself look at her. He wasn't sure he'd be able to keep himself from snarling at her—or worse, kissing her until all of this ugly truth faded away. "I think we've put on quite enough of a show for one night."

She tried to extricate herself from his grip, then scowled at him when he didn't give her an inch as he pulled her along with him down the stairs, through the swirling snow and toward the dock.

"So near-public sex is fine, but heaven forbid anyone overhear an argument?" Lily demanded. She balked when they approached the boat, digging her heels into the slippery dock surface, but he kept moving and therefore, so did she. It was that or let him drag her, and he wasn't surprised she chose the former. "I'm not going anywhere with you. You must be insane!"

"I am a long way past insane, Lily," Rafael said, and

he saw her eyes go wide at his tone, soft and lethal. He leaned in close, holding her gaze with his, and made no attempt at all to hide his dark, seething fury. "I mourned you. I missed you. My life was little more than mausoleum erected to your memory, and it was all a lie. A lie you told by your purposeful absence for years and then, when I found you completely by accident, you told deliberately, to my face."

He could feel her shake beneath his hand, and he didn't think it was that same heat that had worked in her before, that shimmering need he knew as well as his own. He could see that complicated storm in her blue eyes, in the way her lovely mouth trembled and hinted at her reasons, and he didn't want this. Any of this. He'd spent five years dreaming of her return to him, safe and unharmed and his again, but he'd never spent much time worrying about how that might happen. He wasn't sure he wanted to know.

Maybe there were some doors better left closed.

"Rafael—" she began, with a catch in her voice that would be his undoing, if he let it. He refused to let it. And this wasn't the place, no matter what.

He didn't quite bare his teeth as he cut her off.

"If I were you, I'd get in the goddamned boat."

CHAPTER SEVEN

THE BOAT RIDE back across the canal was tense and silent.
The snow fell around them like the kind of holiday blessing
neither one of them deserved, muffling out the sounds of
the old city and transforming it, making it that much more
serene. But far worse than that, Lily thought darkly as she
wrapped her warm cape tightly around her bare shoulders
and glared out at the world become a literal snow globe,
the ride across the water was entirely too brief.

She'd revealed herself at last. Lily had no idea what
that meant, only that it was done and there was no taking it back.

Much too soon, Rafael led her from the boat and into the
waiting loggia level of his family's palazzo, his temper a
living thing that walked beside them, between them, thicker
than the Venice night all around them and stronger than
the hand wrapped around her arm. It didn't occur to her
to defy him. She didn't imagine it would do her any good.

And if she was honest with herself, Lily knew that as
much as she'd tried to avoid this moment of unfortunate
truth, a far deeper part of her was glad. Not that she'd
succumbed to that destructive passion again, the way she
always did like the addict she was—but that there would
be no more lies.

She told herself that was a good thing, as she handed

off her cape to the waiting servant and shivered—though not because she was cold. It was time for honesty, however ugly. It was past time.

Rafael strode through the collection of rooms on the second level, more commonly rented out for things like art exhibits these days than for giving parties like the one they'd just left, then up the stairs she'd come down what seemed like a lifetime ago to the private family living suites above. He kept that seemingly polite hand anchored in the small of her back, guiding her where he wanted her to go, and somehow she didn't quite dare disobey him. Not when she sensed he was holding on the pretense of civility by the skin of his teeth, if that. When a glance at his set, hard face made her think of wild and untamed things, uncontrollable passions, and challenges she hoped she was too wise these days to take.

She hoped.

He ushered her into the vast common room in the center of the bedroom suites that rambled over the upper floor, commanding views of lovely, snowy Venice in all directions. Then he left her standing there in the center of all that opulent art and ancient craft, from the frescoes that adorned the walls to the stunning sweep of paintings to the elegance of the furnishings themselves. An excessive example of the Castelli wealth—and its power—in a single overwarm room, with the brooding fury of Rafael at its center. She watched him stride over to the carved wood cabinet that served as a bar in the corner and pour himself something rich and dark into a heavy-looking tumbler. He tossed it back, then poured himself another, and only then did he turn to face her.

Only then did Lily fully comprehend that she'd simply stood there where he'd left her, like a windup doll waiting to be played with again. Or as if she was awaiting his judgment. As if she deserved his condemnation—but she shied away from that thought almost as soon as it formed.

Rafael was not the victim here. Neither was she. Or they both were, perhaps, and of the same wild passion.

And she told herself that the fact she was still standing there had nothing to do with that glimpse of something like hurt she thought she'd seen on his face when he'd come after her on the steps of the palazzo across the canal. So dark and tormented, and she knew she'd put that there. She knew she'd done that to him, no matter who was the victim here.

Lily had left him, and in the worst way imaginable. That was undeniable. Why should she care if knowing what she'd done hurt him? Hadn't she already hurt him—and everyone else she knew? What could one more hurt matter, set against all the rest?

But she found she was pressing the heel of her hand against her chest, as if that might make it—*her*—feel less hollow.

"Take off that mask," he rasped at her, and the great room they stood in felt closer. Tighter all around her, as if he could control the walls themselves with that terrible voice. "It's time to face each other, after all this time. Don't you think?"

And the truth was, Lily had forgotten she wore the mask at all. Just as she'd forgotten how cold it had been outside until now, when the heat wrapped around her and made her chilled skin seem obvious. Almost painful. She thought there was some shade of meaning in that, as if even the weather was conspiring with Rafael, forcing her to feel all the things she'd vowed she'd never feel again.

But it was time for the truth. For honesty, however brutal.

She pulled the mask from her face and cast it down on the nearest settee that sat with its high back facing her, and she told herself there was no reason whatsoever she should feel vulnerable, suddenly, without it. How had it protected her? The truth was, it hadn't. She could still feel his possession like a pulsing brand between her legs, hot and wild.

He hadn't touched her mask. He'd taken her instead.

And she'd let him. She'd more than *let* him—she'd encouraged him.

Neither one of them had caused this mad thing between them, she knew that. They were both its victim. They were both equally lost in it. They always had been.

"Now," Rafael said, when she looked at him again, still in that voice far darker than the snowy December night at the windows. "Explain."

"You already know what happened."

"No." He looked something more than simply angry. Something more, too, than *hurt*, and she felt that like a fluttering unease deep in her belly. "I know that you died, supposedly. And I know that I then saw you years later on a street in a funny little corner of America. I have drawn conclusions about what must have happened between those two events while you were busy playing identity games, but no. I do not know what happened." She saw his hand tighten around his glass. She felt it as if it had tightened around her, instead. "I certainly don't know *why*."

Lily had spent five years trying to answer these questions to her own satisfaction—but it was something else to answer to *him*. To Rafael, who was the reason behind all of the terrible decisions she'd made in her life, one way or another. She swallowed, found her throat dry and tucked her arms beneath her chest as if that could bolster her against him. Or against this story she'd never wanted to tell.

She still didn't.

"Maybe it's better to let these things lie," she suggested, shocked that her voice sounded so small. She cleared her throat, tried to stand taller. "Please remember that I didn't want to be found."

"Believe me, I remember." His voice was a lash. He swirled the liquid in his glass, his dark eyes on her, and she had the distinct impression he could see all the fine hairs on the back of her neck and along her arms stand up. "And you are stalling."

"What does it matter why?" She fought to sound calm, no matter what she might feel inside. "What can knowing *why* do except make things worse?"

"You let me think you were dead," he hurled at her, and she realized as he did how much he'd been holding back before, out there on the canal. He wasn't restraining himself now, and it took everything she had to keep from flinching away from all that rough emotion. "You let the whole world think you were dead. What kind of person would visit her own death on the people who loved her?"

"You didn't love me," she threw back at him before she had time to temper that. He stiffened, but it was said. There was no taking it back. And besides, it was true. This was about truth. "You were obsessed. You were addicted, maybe. To the secrecy. To the twistedness. To the sheer delight in all the sneaking around and the excitement of all that passion. I know. I was there. But love? No."

"You've done enough, I think, without lecturing me on how I felt."

"I know what you felt," she retorted. "I felt what you felt."

"Evidently not," he gritted out. "Or you would not have sent a car over the side of a cliff and walked away from the wreckage, leaving me to imagine your horrible, painful death forever. You did not feel what I felt, Lily. I rather doubt you feel anything at all."

That stung, but she stood tall and took it. She waited

until her heart felt less painful in her chest as it beat. Until she could speak without that betraying thickness clogging up her throat.

"I felt too much," she told him. "Too much of everything. Too much to bear."

His lips pressed flat, and his gaze was a dark condemnation far worse than anything he could have said. "You'll forgive me if I am unconvinced. Your actions speak their own truth, Lily."

"And what of yours?"

"*I loved you.*" He didn't shout that, either, not quite, and yet Lily thought it rattled the walls, made the whole palazzo shake on its uncertain foundation. "I have never been whole since."

"I think you've fallen in love with a ghost," she told him, her voice shaking slightly. "In retrospect." He made a rough noise, but she ignored it and kept going. "You had five years to make your lost Lily up in your head. Was she virtuous and pure? Did you love her so desperately no living woman can compare? Was her loss a blow from which you've never quite recovered?" She shrugged when he scowled at her. "She sounds like a paragon. But that's not me, Rafael. And that was certainly not you."

"I loved you," he gritted out again, and though he was quieter this time, she still felt it slam through her. "You can't make that go away because it isn't convenient for you."

"I remember exactly how you loved me, Rafael," she told him in the same sort of voice, holding herself tightly in check, as if that might keep her safe from all these truths filling the room. "I remember all the women you slept with while you claimed we had to remain a secret. You said you had to maintain your cover. You laughed when it upset me. Tell me, did you love me this much while you were inside them?"

And for a moment Lily didn't know which was worse—the possibility that he wouldn't answer her…or that he would.

"If this is your version of an explanation, it's terrible," he snarled at her after a long beat, and then he tossed back the contents of his glass in a single smooth motion. He slapped the tumbler down on the cabinet behind him with a loud *crack* that made Lily jump. "I'm not the liar in this room."

"On the contrary," she replied, hoping there was none of that jumpiness in her voice. "There are two liars in this room. You're not the story you've been telling yourself, Rafael."

"Is this the real Lily talking now or this ghost I made up in my head?" he asked, his dark gaze glittering with fury. "I'm finding it difficult to keep track."

She shook her head at him. "Liars are all we've ever been, starting that first night when you took my virginity on a pile of coats in the guest room of your father's château and then strolled back into the party to kiss your girlfriend at midnight as if it had never happened." Lily laughed softly at his expression, not sure where the will to do so came from, when he looked so fierce. "I'm sorry, had you prettied that up in your imagination? Made it all wine and roses and no cheating or sneaking around? Well, that wasn't us. And I'm as bad as you are, make no mistake, because I knew perfectly well you had a girlfriend and I didn't try to stop it."

He stared at her, all outraged male and dark ruthlessness besides, and she watched as that sank in. As it moved through him. And she'd imagined this moment so many times. She'd envisioned bludgeoning him with the truth and that changing everything, somehow.

But instead she felt worse. Incalculably worse.

"We were terrible people," she said then, with an urgency that made her voice shake slightly.

"We must have been," he said as he moved toward her, a kind of bleakness in his voice she'd never heard before. "Look at where we are."

"Maybe," she told him, her voice low, "you should have let us both forget."

He shook his head, an expression she'd never seen before moving over his dark face.

"But that's the problem, isn't it? Neither one of us has forgotten a thing."

That felt like a dig. Lily stiffened. "That doesn't mean we have to wallow in the past."

"Is that what you think this is?" Rafael asked. He shrugged, an edgy movement that did nothing to mask that thunderous, broken thing in his gaze. "Maybe so. But I'm not going to apologize for how I mourned you, Lily. How I coped with your loss. You walked away. You knew what you were doing. I didn't have that choice."

"Your choices came before that," she retorted, stung and hurt and furious at the both of them, that all of this could still hurt like this after so much time had passed. After so much had changed. "And you chose secrets. Lies. Other women."

"I won't deny that I was a selfish man, Lily," he bit out, his gaze like fire, and she didn't know when he'd ventured so close to her. "I can't. I regret it every day. But we had no commitment. I may not have treated you as well as I should have, but I didn't betray you."

She pulled in a breath, amazed at the burst of white-hot pain that caused when there was nothing fresh or new in this. Nothing but an old wound, a dull blade.

And the same familiar hand to wield it.

"Of course you didn't." She wished she could hate him.

She truly did. Surely that would be better. Simpler. "Oh, and along those lines, I never concealed Arlo from you. Technically. Had I seen you, I would have told you."

That shimmered in the air between them, like anguish.

If she could die from this, Lily thought, she would have already. Years ago. God knew, she'd come close.

Rafael said something harsh in Italian, vicious and low. He hauled her to him with a wholly inelegant hand around her neck, sending her sprawling into his hard chest. Then he stopped talking and took her mouth with his.

And this time, there was no party nearby. No parents who might be horrified at what their stepprogeny were about. No one to walk in on them. No one to hear.

This time, Rafael took his time.

He kissed her like this really was love. Like she'd been wrong all along. His mouth was condemnation and caress at once, taking her over and drawing her near, and Lily lost herself the way she always did.

Heedless. Hungry. Needy and desperate and entirely his.

Just as it had always been.

Rafael shrugged his way out of his coat, letting it drop to the thick carpet beneath them, and still he kissed her. He sank his hands deep into her hair, scattering the combs that held it in place until the heavy mass of it tumbled down around them and the sparkling accessories rained out across the floor, and still he stroked her tongue with his, deeper and more intense, as if nothing in the world could ever matter as much as the delirious friction of his mouth against hers.

Lily traced the planes of his chest, unable to control herself and not certain she wanted to try. She dug her fingers into the gaps between his buttons and pulled, gratified when the buttons burst free and exposed the smooth, hard planes of his sculpted chest. And then she succumbed to that same old need and ran her palms against his hot, smooth skin like red-hot steel with its dusting of dark hair. She was aware of his scent, soap and Rafael, his devil's mouth teasing hers to endless wickedness, and the truth of her own mounting desire for this man she shouldn't want like a near-painful ache low in her belly.

She wrenched her mouth from his and they both panted as they stared at each other, all the twisted wrongness of their connection, all the lies they'd told and the things they'd done, like a thick mist between them, blurring the edges of things.

He said something despairing in Italian that hurt to hear, and she didn't even understand the words. Lily didn't know what to do. It was easier to hurl old, embittered words at him. It was easier to try to hate him.

It was so very easy to hate herself, lecture herself on the importance of abstinence, call herself an addict. But heroin didn't feel pain in return. Heroin didn't *hurt*.

It was infinitely harder to tilt her head closer and to press her lips into the hollow between his pectoral muscles, like the apology she didn't dare utter. That she was afraid to admit she wanted to speak out loud at all.

Rafael sighed, or perhaps it was a groan, and tore the rest of his shirt off without her having to ask. And then he stood there, bared to the waist, even more perfect than he'd been all these years inside her head.

She couldn't read the look on his face then, nor define what rose in her in response. What tore at her and threatened to rip her apart, and it was all there in the dark gold of his eyes. In the constriction in her chest, making her wonder if she'd ever really breathe again.

"Turn around," he ordered her. She froze, but he only stared back at her implacably, his eyes too dark and too bright. "Do not make me repeat myself."

She obeyed without quite meaning to, turning so her back was to him and she faced the scrolled height of the nearby settee.

"Rafael—" she began, but cut herself off on a sharp intake of breath when he came up hard behind her, that mighty chest of his pressed into her back, making her feel dizzy with need.

That endless, delirious, life-altering need.

"These are your choices, Lily." His mouth was close enough to that sensitive place just behind her ear that she could feel the tickle of it, a sharp, impossible electricity that seemed to bolt straight through her to linger in her core. She was surrounded by him, sex and scent and strength, and she didn't know what she felt. Who she was anymore, when she was with him. What the hell she was doing. But she also couldn't seem to stop. "You can walk away right now, go to sleep, dream of all the ways we've wronged each other so we can tear bigger chunks from each other in the morning. I won't blame you if you do."

She felt as if she couldn't breathe, but that was her, she understood, making that rough sound. That harsh breathing a little too close to outright panting.

"Or...?" she asked, in a voice that hardly sounded like hers.

But it was. She knew it was.

So did Rafael.

And he was hard and hot and perfect behind her. "Or you can bend over that settee and hold on tight."

Rafael expected her to bolt. To take a breath and then hurl herself away from him. Run screaming from him. Maybe some part of him wanted her to do exactly that.

Maybe he didn't know which one of them he was trying to scare.

He heard the deep, shuddering breath she took. He braced himself for her to walk away. Told himself that he would let her. That he had no other choice.

"And…" She shifted from one foot to the other. "And what happens if I do that?"

He didn't pretend he didn't know which *that* she meant. Triumph lashed at him, more potent than the whiskey he'd tossed back, and he smiled. Hard.

His hand smoothed down the length of her side, all that silken heat and the tattoo he knew waited for him beneath her dress. She bucked slightly against him, then went too still, as if she couldn't control herself any better than he could.

And he found that made all the difference. It clarified things.

It didn't matter how messy this was. What they'd lost. How they'd lied.

It didn't make her any less his.

Nothing could.

"Bend over, Lily," he ordered her, as gruff as he was certain, and he was animal enough to enjoy the trembling reaction he could see her fight to repress when he said it. "Now."

CHAPTER EIGHT

LILY STEPPED AWAY from him, and Rafael found he hardly breathed as she stood there for a moment, as if she hadn't quite made up her mind. Not quite yet. She shifted her weight again and he heard the faint rustle of her skirt like a shout before she twisted around to look over her shoulder at him.

Her eyes were so blue. Like that fathomless California sky. He'd thought he'd never see them again, that marvelous color. He'd had to content himself with memory. He'd had to settle for lesser blues, minor marvels.

He wasn't going to settle again.

Rafael had a thousand things he wanted to say to her, but none of that mattered when what they boiled down to was the same thing: she was his. No matter the distance, the years. The hurts lodged and the lies told. What she thought of him, them, the past, the future they'd have to work out now that there was Arlo to consider. That was all noise.

Lily was the sweet, deep quiet at the center of all of that. *She was his.*

He saw her breathe in, then let it out. He saw her decision flash in her gorgeous eyes, a resolve that lifted her chin again and made every part of him clench tight in anticipation and a spark of something much too close to fear—

She turned away from him again and took another step, then bent herself forward, gripping the back of the settee the way he'd told her to do.

Lust and need and a deep kick of pure triumph punched into him then. So hard it hollowed him out. He wanted her so badly in that moment that if he touched her, he imagined he'd simply implode. And that wouldn't do at all.

So instead, he made her wait.

He went back over to the bar and poured himself another drink. He took his time with it, watching her intently.

"Do not move," he ordered her, more silk than reprimand, when he saw her shift as if she meant to straighten. "It is your turn to wait, Lily. I waited for five years with no hope that you would ever return. You've waited five seconds so far and you know exactly where I am. You can suffer the unknown a little while longer, don't you think?"

"I didn't know you were into torture," she retorted, and he could see her defiance in the way she braced herself against the ornate little settee, too fussy to be a couch. The way she tilted her head to one side, sending all that heavy, slippery strawberry blond hair of hers cascading over one shoulder. "Is that a new hobby?"

"You have no idea," he murmured.

"You could simply kiss me like a normal person," she pointed out, almost chattily, as if she wasn't standing there in a remarkably provocative position, awaiting his pleasure. "Or is that too pedestrian for a Castelli heir in a Venetian palazzo?"

"Ogni volta che ti bacio dimentico dove sono." Every time I kiss you I forget where I am. He hadn't meant to say that.

But the truth was, he didn't simply want this woman. He admired her. He craved her sharp tongue as much as he wanted to feel the wet heat of it against his skin. He had never managed to reconcile himself to the loss of her. He had been made a different man entirely by her loss—and he didn't know, now, how to pull those different pieces of himself together into one again. If that was even possible.

He set his drink back down untouched and roamed back toward her, eyeing the picture she made as she waited there with the dress the color of the sea all around her and her exquisite form within it like some kind of mythical creature, too perfect to be believed. Yet this was Venice, after all. It was easier to believe all things were possible in a city that should not exist, propped up like so many dreams nailed fast to alder trees and left in the sea for centuries.

But Lily was here again, wasn't she? She lived, as his brother had pointed out to him. She had not died in that car accident. This was not a dream, despite the many, many times he'd had dreams just like it. Rafael could call this—*her*—a miracle if he chose, and he told himself he would worry later over the vicious little details that had made it all possible.

Much later.

He leaned over her, into her, caging her where she stood with his hands on either side of hers. She shuddered in that deep, luxuriant way that seemed to roll all the way through her and then into him, and when he bent to press his mouth to the nape of her neck, they both sighed.

She was so warm, so delicately fragrant. He could smell that particular scent that was only hers, a sultry blend of her skin and her sex, and layered over that the hints of bathing products and stylist's tools, cosmetics and the faint touch of something not quite slate that made him think of the snow outside.

And the skin beneath his lips was so soft. So very soft. She shivered, and he wanted to inhale her. All of her.

"*La tua pelle e' come seta,*" Rafael murmured, right

there against that sensitive spot at her nape, knowing full well she couldn't understand him. Enjoying that fact, if he was honest. *Your skin is like silk.*

"Why can't I turn around?" Her voice was little more than a breath.

He smiled against her skin. "Because this way, there can only be honesty between us. No harsh words to confuse the issue. No lies or make-believe memories. You will either respond to me or you won't."

"You don't seem worried that I won't," she said, almost ruefully.

He grazed her lightly with his teeth and heard the sharp little noise she made in response, music to him the way it always had been, and he leaned in closer and indulged himself.

"No," he said against her soft, warm skin, "I'm not."

Rafael laid a trail of fire down the length of her neck, then across the delicate ridges of her finely wrought shoulder blades. He explored one with his mouth, his hands, then the other. He kept her caged there by his much larger body, drinking in every little sweet and helpless sound she made—far more intoxicating than any whiskey.

And only when he'd relearned every sweet inch of her upper back did he pull back. She was shuddering again, her head low between her shoulders, breathing as hard as if she'd been running.

"You might want to brace yourself, *cara*," he told her, making no attempt to hide the sheer male satisfaction in his voice. "I'm only getting started."

He heard a hitch in her breath and it took him a moment to realize it was a laugh. Low, husky. Infinitely sensual. It wrapped around him and pierced his bones, shaking through him like a quiet little tsunami.

"Promises, promises," she taunted him softly.

She was lethal. Rafael would do well to remember that.

He reached out then and found the hidden zipper closure of her dress, unhooking it and then beginning to pull it down, exposing the long line of her spine and the acres of her soft skin. His mouth watered, but still he unzipped her, letting the dress fall from her mouthwatering curves to foam around her feet, effectively caging her there in yards and yards of fabric so soft to the touch that the only thing that could possibly be softer was her.

She was like a feast spread before him, and he let himself breathe her in, exposed at last to his view. His own personal miracle. He took in the wavy tangle of her strawberry blond hair, the elegance of her lovely back and the scrap of scarlet he'd shoved out of his way at the party that was, from this angle, a mere hint of fabric circling her hips and then disappearing between the high, proud curves of her bottom. Then he took his time on the way back up, lingering on that tattoo he'd believed he'd never see again, that tattoo that had proved she was who he knew her to be at a glance, that tattoo that marked her *his Lily* forever.

He touched her there, tracing the winding black lines that curled this way and that, the tendrils reaching down almost to the top of her thong panties at the bottom and then nearly to what would have been her bra line, had she been wearing one, at the top. Then he worked his fingers over the delicate lily blossom some stranger had lovingly drawn into her skin, the arched petals and the sweet bud within, as if he was painting her with his possession.

"Rafael..." Her voice cracked on his name, and he smiled at the raw need in it. "Please."

"Please, what?" he asked. "I've hardly begun. And I think this tattoo is yet another lie you've told."

She shook her head, lifting herself up but still, he noticed, maintaining her position. Staying where he'd put her, and he didn't know what made him want her more, her obedience or her need. Both.

"A tattoo is the opposite of a lie," she said, still in that breathy, needy way of hers that was messing with his resolve. "It's ink on skin and unchangeable."

"And if you hated it as much as you claimed you did," he murmured as he leaned in closer, then sank down so he could set his mouth against the center bud of that pretty red blossom, "you would have had it removed by now."

He heard her shudder out another breath that was edging toward a sob, and he continued to taste that delicate flower while he let his hands wander, smoothing their way over her hips and then testing the sweet curves of her bottom. And only when he could feel her shake did he tease his way into the hidden hollow beneath, where she was molten and hot and more than ready for him.

Rafael knew her body better than his own. He knew her taste, her shape. He knew exactly how to touch her to drive her slowly, slowly insane. And if it killed him too, well— resurrections were going around. He was certain he'd survive, somehow, if only to find her again. He stroked his way into her heat, tracing her folds and the center of her need until she was surging back to meet him.

"Tell me something," he said darkly, moving as he spoke from the sweet tattoo to the sweep of her spine, relearning that perfect curve, that tempting shape. "How many men did Alison have in those five years?"

He could feel her stiffen at that, but he had two fingers deep inside her, and there was only one truth that had ever mattered between them. It didn't matter what he said to her, or what lies she told. It didn't matter how furious she was with him or what she'd done. What he'd done with all those other women, for that matter, or how much he regretted every one of them. He could feel her, molten and sweet, clenching tight around him even so.

This was the only truth. This heat. This need. This was who they were.

"You're a hypocrite," she panted out, sounding as desperate as she did furious, and yet her hips moved in wild abandon, meeting every stroke. "You must know that."

"I have never claimed otherwise," he said, his voice rough. "Especially not to you. But that doesn't answer my question, does it?"

"What does it matter?" she demanded, and then she let out a small cry when he changed his angle and drove deeper within her. Harder.

"How many?"

He felt her shudder beneath him, and he stopped pretending he was anything but an animal where this woman was concerned. Or that he'd ever been anything else. Or would ever be anything else. Five years apart, thinking she was dead, hadn't changed this. Nothing could.

"Tell me," he gritted out at her.

"None, Rafael," she cried out as he pressed hard against the center of her hunger with one hand and stroked deep with the other. "There has never been anyone but you."

And there never will be, he thought, feeling something clawed and fierce inside him, fighting its way out through his rib cage.

"For that," he said, moving up higher and setting his mouth against her ear, exulting in the way she bucked and writhed beneath him, "you get a reward."

Then he twisted his hand and hit her in precisely the right spot, and held her as she broke apart.

And he was only getting started.

* * *

Lily hardly registered it when he lifted her, sweeping her out of the dress that was now crumpled on the floor and up into his arms. But she did feel the change in temperature when he strode through the doors of the great room and out into the hall, holding her high against his bare chest.

She should have been cold, she knew, but what she felt instead was something like cherished, in nothing but her thong with her hair trailing over his arm. *Safe*, a small voice inside her whispered. The way it always had when she was with this man—the very last man who could ever be considered even remotely safe.

But Lily hooked her arms around his neck and didn't ask herself any questions.

Rafael shouldered his way through another set of doors, and Lily only had a moment to take in a sitting room lit by cheerful little lamps made of colorful glass before he'd walked straight through it and into a majestic bedroom set high above the Grand Canal. She saw the glittering lights of the old buildings outside and the snow that fell all around, and then the world narrowed down to the canopied four-poster bed that dominated the richly patterned room. Paintings framed in gold graced the solemn red walls, there was a dancing fire in the massive fireplace on the far wall, and there was Rafael in the center of everything.

He set her down at the side of the great bed, his expression unreadable. Her hair hung around her in a great mess, and she was naked while he still wore the bottom half of his dark suit. Lily thought that any one of those things should have bothered her, but they didn't.

She could sense all the things she *ought* to have felt dancing all around her, just out of sight. As if, were she to turn her head fast enough, she'd see them there, waiting to pounce. But she didn't turn her head. She couldn't seem to tear her gaze away from Rafael's.

"You remember me," he said then, after what felt like a very long while.

It could have been an accusation—but it wasn't. He lifted his hand and held it out and she matched it with hers, laying it against his in that small space between them, so they were palm to palm.

"Yes," she said softly, aware that it sounded like a vow in the quiet of the vast room. "I remember you. I remember this."

It was easier to remember the wild highs and the dark lows, she knew. All the sex and the lies, the betrayals and the fights. But that hadn't been the sum total of what had passed between them. The truth was, Lily didn't like to remember the other part. It still hurt too much.

But that didn't seem to matter now, in a fairy tale of a bedchamber in this magical city, while the snow kept falling and the fire danced, and he was right there in front of her and far more beautiful than she'd let herself remember.

She'd been nineteen that New Year's Eve. She'd taunted him and he'd taken her and then they'd walked back into their lives and pretended nothing had happened. He'd played the attentive boyfriend to whatever silly girlfriend he'd had then. She'd pretended to be as disgusted with him and the entire Castelli family as she always had been.

Then the holiday had passed, and it had been time for her to head back to Berkeley, to carry on with her sophomore year of college. He'd caught up to her in the grand front foyer of the château as she'd headed out toward her car with her bags. His girlfriend had been laughing it up in the next room with the rest of their families. They could have been discovered at any moment.

Rafael hadn't spoken. He'd hardly looked at her since New Year's Eve. But he'd held out his hand like this, and she'd met it. And it had felt a lot like crying, that heaviness within, that constriction and that ache, all bound up in such a simple touch. But they'd stood like that for what had felt like a very long time.

Now, all these years later, Lily understood it better. This was their connection in its least destructive form. This touch. This *thing*. It still arced between them, tying them together, rendering all the rest of what they were unimportant beside it.

"I thought I'd lost you," he said quietly, so quietly she almost thought she'd imagined it. But then his dark eyes met hers and held. "I thought you were gone forever."

The sheer brutality of what she'd done hit her, then. She'd understood she'd hurt him, yes. She'd hurt a lot of people. She'd told herself she'd accepted that, and that Arlo was worth it. But she'd never thought about *this*. The warmth of his flesh against hers. This connection of theirs that defied all thought, all reason, all efforts to squash it. What would she have done if she'd thought he'd died? How could she possibly have lived with that?

Her throat was too tight to speak. She didn't try. Instead, she leaned forward and pressed a kiss in the center of his chest. She felt his breath rush out, but she didn't stop. She pushed him back against the bed, aware that he let her move him like that, that she couldn't have shifted his powerful frame if he hadn't allowed it.

She still couldn't speak. But that didn't mean she couldn't apologize in her way.

Lily poured her sorrow and her regret all over him, making it into heat. He leaned back on his hands and she crawled over him, pressing kisses down the strong column of his throat, over that strong, hard pulse that she knew beat for her, then lower, to celebrate the sheer masculine perfection of his chest. She let her hair slip this way and that as she slid down the length of him, tasting him and celebrating him, pouring herself over him like sunlight until she unbuckled his trousers, pulled them down, then shoved them out of her way.

She paused then, flicking a look at him as she took his hard length in her hands. His gaze was black with need, his face set in stark and glorious lines of pure hunger, and apology merged with simple desire as she bent and sucked him deep into her mouth.

Rafael groaned. Or maybe that was her name.

Lily sank down between his legs, reveling in him. The taste of his hardness, salt and man. Satin poured over steel, and he trembled faintly the more she played with him, the deeper she took him.

He sank his hands in her hair and held her there as she taunted him with her tongue then took him deep yet again. He murmured Italian phrases that sounded like prayers but were, she knew, words of sex and need. Encouragement and stark male approval.

"Enough."

His voice was so gruff she hardly recognized it, but she understood it when he pulled her from him and lifted her against him, rolling them back and onto the wide bed. For a moment she thought he would simply take over, but he rolled once more, settling her there on top of him so he nudged up against her slick folds.

His gaze was like fire, or maybe the fire was in her. Maybe this was all fire.

She reached between them and took him in her hand. She felt his swift intake of breath, or perhaps it was a curse, and then they both groaned when she shifted and took him deep inside her.

Naked, she thought, as if the word was an incantation. Or a prayer.

They were both naked. This wasn't a coatroom, an alcove outside a dance or any of the other semipublic places they'd done this over the years. This was no illicit hotel room when they'd both claimed to be somewhere else. No one was looking for them and even if they were, it wouldn't matter if they were found.

This was simply them, skin to skin, at last.

And then Lily began to move.

That same fire burned high, but this was a sweeter blaze. The pace she set was lazy. Dangerous. Rafael lay beneath her, his hands at her hips, his gaze locked to hers.

Perfect, Lily thought. *He has always been perfect.*

And then she rode them both right off the side of the earth, and into bliss.

CHAPTER NINE

LILY WOKE TO find herself all alone in that great bed, the sheets a tangle below her and the canopy like a filmy tent high above.

For a moment, she couldn't remember where she was.

It came back to her slowly at first, then with a great rush. That quick plane ride down from the remote lake in the Dolomites yesterday afternoon, then the boat that had whisked them through the eerie, echoing wonder of the Venice canals, past winding, narrow byways and under more than one distractingly elegant bridge. After which she'd spent hours getting ready for a ball she hadn't wanted to attend in the first place, surrounded by servants like some kind of latter-day queen, finding herself less and less averse to the night ahead the more she liked the way they made her look in the beveled mirror in front her.

There was the most unpalatable truth of all: that she really was that vain.

But it had been worth it when she'd seen that stunned, famished look on Rafael's face as she'd made her way down the long stair to his side. It had all been worth it.

Looking back, Lily thought she could trace all the rest of her questionable decisions last night to that moment. The long walk down, her gaze fastened to his, while he looked at her as if she was the answer to a very fervent prayer.

She sat up slowly now, the long night evident in the small tugs and pulls all over her body, unable to regret a single one of them. She imagined that would come. But in the meantime, she rolled from the bed and drew the coverlet around her as she stood. The fire was low in the grate, while the thin light of dawn made the air seem blue. Rafael was nowhere to be found and when she cocked her head to listen intently, she couldn't hear him in the bath suite either. Outside, last night's snow dusted all the boats moored along the edges of the canal and the tops of the grand palazzos opposite, making a particularly Venetian Christmas card out of the already lovely view.

Lily placed her hand against the glass the same way she'd placed it against Rafael's hand the night before, felt that deep ache in her heart, and understood entirely too many things at once.

She was in love with him. Of course she was. She had always been in love with him, and it was as wretched a thing now as it had been when she'd been nineteen.

Because nothing had changed. Not really.

They were the same people they had always been and now the past five years were between them. And Arlo. And all the sex in the world, no matter how good, couldn't change what she'd done or who Rafael was or any of the many, many reasons they could never, ever work.

At heart he was his father, who married and remarried at the drop of a hat and believed himself deeply in love without ever having to prove it for too long. And she was entirely too much like her own mother, who had disappeared into the things she loved, whether they were prescription drugs or men—until it had killed her. So selfish. So destructive.

Running away in the way she had might not have been a particularly mature choice, or even a good one. Lily understood that. The pain she'd caused was incalculable. One night in Venice couldn't change that. Maybe nothing could.

She was no less selfish. No less destructive. But at least she was aware of it; she accepted the truth about her behavior, however unpleasant. Like everything else, she thought then, there was nothing to do but live with it. One way or another.

She squared her shoulders and dropped her chilled hand back down from the window, feeling scraped raw inside. Lily decided that was hunger. She couldn't remember the last time she'd eaten something. She pushed her way out of the bedroom into the sitting room she'd glimpsed so haphazardly last night, sure there must be something to eat somewhere in a palace so grand.

But she stopped short when she entered the sitting room. The fire in here was blazing, and there was an impressive selection of breakfast foods laid out along the side table as she'd expected, but what caught her attention was Rafael.

He stood by the windows, looking out on what she assumed was the same view she'd left behind in the other room. She thought that was the sum total of who they were. Forever separated, forever lost to each other in pursuit of the same end. A wave of melancholy threatened to take her from her feet then, surprising her with its strength.

She shoved it back down and blinked that heat in her eyes away.

"It's pretty out there," she said, inanely, and it was worse because her throat was so raw. She coughed and pulled the coverlet tighter around her, cold despite the warmth of the room. "Though very raw, I think. With all that snow."

It had something to do with the way Rafael stood there, so remote, wearing nothing but low-slung trousers that showed off that powerful body of his. It was the set of his broad shoulders, or that sense that he wasn't really there at all. That he saw something other than the snow and the canal, and the light of a winter morning turning the sky to liquid gold.

"My mother was mad," he said without turning around, as if he was wholly impervious to the cold on the other side of that window. Or in his own voice. "That is not the preferred term, I know. There were so many diagnoses, so many suppositions. But in the end, mad is what she was, no matter how they tried to sanitize it."

· All it had taken was an internet connection to find the few articles about Gianni Castelli's doomed first marriage, so this was not precisely news to Lily. She'd read everything she could in a fury when she'd been sixteen and less than pleased about her mother's new fiancé. But she couldn't remember Rafael ever discussing his family history before. Not ever, in all the time she'd known him. That he was choosing to do so now, unprompted, made her heart beat hard and low in her chest.

"That is the excuse that was always trotted out in those years before she was taken away," he said after a moment, when Lily didn't respond. "That she was sick. Unwell. That she wasn't responsible for her actions." He shifted then, turning to look at her, though that wasn't an improvement. That darkly gorgeous face of his was shuttered. Hard. Her heart kicked that much harder against her ribs. "As it turns out, it's not much of an excuse when it's your mother they're talking about."

"What did she do?" Lily didn't know how she dared to speak. She realized she'd stopped dead a step from the door, and forced herself to move again. She walked farther into the deceptively cheery room and perched on the edge of the nearest chaise, as if she couldn't feel the terrible tension in the air.

"Nothing," Rafael said softly, his dark eyes bleak on hers. "She did absolutely nothing."

Lily swallowed, hard. "I don't know what that means."

His mouth shifted into something not at all a smile. "It means she did nothing, Lily. When we fell. When we ran to her. When we jockeyed for her attention, when we ignored her. It was all the same. She acted as if she was alone. Perhaps, in her mind, she was."

"I'm sorry." Lily didn't know why he was telling her this story, and she couldn't read any clues on his face. "That can't have been easy."

"Eventually she was whisked away to a hospital in Switzerland," he continued in the same distant tone. "At first we visited her there. I think my father must have believed that she could be fixed, you see. He's always liked to put broken things back together. But my mother could not be repaired, no matter how many drugs or therapies or exciting new regimens they tried. Eventually, they all gave up." He thrust his hands in his pockets, and though he didn't look away from her, Lily wasn't sure he saw her, either. "My father divorced her, claiming that was best for everyone, though it seemed it was really only best for him. The hospital started talking about her comfort and safety rather than her progress, and told us it was better if we stayed away."

Lily didn't know what she meant to say. What she could say. Only that she wanted to help him, heal him somehow, and couldn't. "I'm so sorry."

His mouth moved into a harsh curve. "I was thirteen the last time I saw her. I'd taken the train from my boarding school, filled with all the requisite drama and purpose of a young man on a mission. I had long since determined that my father was to blame for her decline, and that if I could see her alone, I could know the truth. I wanted to *rescue* her."

Lily stared back at him, stricken. The fire popped and crackled beside her, but Rafael didn't appear to hear it. And she couldn't seem to read a single thing on that hard face of his.

"Rafael," she said in a low voice. "You don't have to tell me any of this."

"But I do," he replied. He studied her for a moment, then continued. "The hospital wouldn't let me see her, only observe her from afar. My memories of her were of her rages, her tears. The way she would go blank in the middle of crowded rooms. Yet the woman I saw, alone in her little room, was at peace." He laughed, a hollow sound. "She was *happy* there, locked up in that place. Far happier than she had ever been outside it."

Lily studied him for a moment. "What did you do?"

He shrugged in that supremely Italian way. "What could I do? I was thirteen and she wasn't in need of rescuing. I left her there. Three years later, she was dead. They say she accidentally overdosed on pills she should not have been hoarding. I doubt very much it was an accident. But by then, I had discovered women."

Lily stiffened where she sat, and a harsh sort of light gleamed in his dark eyes, as if he could track her every movement. "I don't understand why you're sharing these things with me."

"I had no intention of becoming my father," Rafael told her quietly. "I had no interest in becoming some kind of relationship mechanic, forever tinkering around beneath the hood of another broken thing. I liked a laugh. I liked sex. I wanted nothing but a good time and when it turned heavy, the way it inevitably did? I was gone. I never wanted to feel that urge to rescue anyone, not ever again. I wanted no complications, no trouble." His gaze was hard on hers, bright and hot. "And then came you."

"You shouldn't have kissed me," she threw at him, as if this was a fight they were having instead of a quiet conversation in a cheerfully cozy room on a snowy December morning.

"No," he murmured, and she might have said it first, but she found she greatly disliked his ready agreement. "I shouldn't have touched you. I had no idea what I was unleashing." She thought he tensed where he stood. Maybe that was how he seemed to crowd out all the air in the room. "And I hated it. I hated you."

She couldn't breathe. "You hated me," she repeated, flatly, as if that would make it hurt less.

"I thought if I could pretend it hadn't happened, it would go away. But it kept happening." That dark, ruthless gaze of his tore her up. It made her shake. But he didn't stop. "I thought if I could contain it, control it, diminish it or dilute it, I could conquer it. Keep it hidden. Choke the life out of it before it swallowed me whole."

"I didn't ask you to tell me any of this," she said then, feeling off balance. Something like dizzy, as if she was propped there on the edge of a cliff instead of an overstuffed chaise. "I wish you would stop."

"But then you went over the side of a cliff you shouldn't have been near, in a car you shouldn't have been driving, going much too fast," he said, his voice hoarse, and she could see from that look in his eyes that he had no intention of stopping. "I knew perfectly well that if you'd been upset, the way they claimed you must have been to drive like that, it was my fault. They said it was an accident, that you'd lost control and skidded, but I wondered. Was it really an accident? Or had I made your life so bloody miserable that your only chance at any kind of happiness was to escape me the only way you could? Just like she did."

She was shaking outright then. "Rafael—"

"Except here you are," he said softly, and she wished he would move. She wished he would *do something* more than simply stand there like some kind of creature of stone, breaking her heart more with every word. "And you still make my breath catch when you enter a room. And I've long since understood that it was never hate I felt for you, but that I was too immature or too afraid to understand the enormity of it any other way. And you have my child, this perfect and beautiful son I thought I didn't want until I met him." He shook his head slightly, as if the reality of Arlo still overwhelmed him. "And I don't hate you, Lily. I want you in ways I've never wanted any other woman. I can't imagine that changing if it hasn't yet. But you're right."

His gaze was so bright, so hard, it hurt. And she'd been turned to stone herself.

"I don't love you," Rafael said. "If I can love anything at all, if I'm capable of such a thing, I love that ghost."

Lily was dimly surprised that she was still in one piece after that. That the building hadn't sunk into the water all around them. That there was still a sun to peek in the windows on this cold, ruined day. That she hadn't simply turned to a column of ash and blown off into nothingness in the next breath.

And he wasn't finished.

"I will always love that ghost," he said, very distinctly, so there could be no mistake. So she could not misunderstand. "She's in my head, my heart, as selfish and as worthless as I might be. Yet it's the flesh and blood woman I can't forgive, Lily. If I'm honest with you, I don't know that I ever will." His smile then was a razor, sad and lethal at once. "But don't worry. I doubt I'll forgive myself."

Rafael watched her take that in, a kaleidoscope of emotion moving over her expressive face, and told himself it wasn't a lie. Not quite. It was the truth—*a* truth. It was just that there was a greater truth he had no intention of sharing with her.

Because he couldn't trust her, no matter the temptation to do exactly that. He knew her better than any other person alive, and he knew her not at all, and he'd understood over the course of that long, blisteringly hot night that he thought was branded into his very flesh that this was exactly the kind of heaviness he'd spent his life avoiding. For good reason.

There were other words for all those weighty things that rolled over him, pressing down on him like some kind of pitiless vise. He wasn't afraid of them any longer. But he'd succumbed to his vulnerabilities last night. He wouldn't do it again. There was Arlo to consider now.

And Rafael would be damned if he would ruin his son's life the way his parents had so cavalierly wrecked his, by betting on *feelings* when it was the practical application of reason and strength that got things done. He'd spent the past five years proving exactly that in his business affairs. He could do no less for his only child.

He wouldn't live his life for the ghost he hadn't saved. He couldn't.

"We are going to have to decide what story we wish to tell," he said coolly, when it looked as if Lily had wrestled her reactions under control. She was wrapped up in that gold thing she must have pulled from his bed, her hair a glorious halo of strawberry blond all around her and falling over her shoulders, and he felt like a saint for maintaining his distance when it was the last thing he wanted to do. But it was necessary. No matter that her blue eyes looked slicked with hurt and it caused him physical pain to know he'd done that to her. Again. "Whatever the version, I have no intention of hiding the fact that I'm Arlo's father. From the world or from him. You need to come to terms with that."

She blinked, and then she rose somewhat stiffly to her feet, and he couldn't tell if that was a remnant of the night they'd shared or if it was an emotional response to the things he'd told her. Or both.

"What do you mean?" she asked, and the gaze she fixed on him was blue and cool, no hint of any hurt or wetness. He was tempted to think he'd imagined it. "I'm in Italy, aren't I? If I hadn't come to terms with it, I imagine I'd still be back home in Virginia, knee-deep in dogs."

"You are in Italy, yes," Rafael said quietly. "Hidden away in a house off in the mountains where no one has seen you or him except a handful of villagers who would never question the family. And then masked in public here, so no one could recognize you. You can't have it both ways for too much longer, I'm afraid."

Lily yanked her gaze from his and moved over to the side table, where she poured herself a cup of coffee with a hand that looked perfectly steady—and a good man, he was aware, would not *want* to see this woman, the mother of his child, so upset she shook. He understood that once again, he'd proved he could never be anything like *good*. Especially not where Lily was involved.

"I don't know why you think a certain reticence is trying to have it both ways," she said after a moment. She glanced at him over her shoulder, looking as though she belonged in the paintings that graced the walls, draped in gold and her own wavy hair. "What story do you think we ought to tell, Rafael? The one you just bludgeoned me with?"

He acknowledged the truth in that with a shrug. "You can't imagine that you can rise from the dead unremarked, can you?"

"I don't see why not," she said, blowing on her coffee and then taking a sip before she turned to face him again. "It's not anybody's business."

"Perhaps not. But the media attention will be unavoidable." He sounded impatient even by his own reckoning, but that coverlet was sliding down her upper arm, now, coming perilously close to shifting just far enough to expose the rosy tip of her breast. He needed to focus. "You died tragically and very young. That you are alive and well and in possession of the heir to the Castelli fortune will make it all that much more irresistible."

She'd become that stranger again, cool and unreadable— or maybe she, too, had grown up in these intervening years. Become less raw, less emotional. Or at least less likely to show her every thought on her face. It was his own curse that he should feel that like a loss. Like one more thing to grieve.

"It sounds like you already know what they'll say," she said mildly. It was her turn to shrug. "Why can't we let them say it?"

"The real story here isn't your unexpected resurrection, as exciting as that might be," he replied after a moment, after he'd had to force himself to look away from her almost-yet-not-quite-revealed breast. "It's the question of what happened five years ago."

"And here I thought rising from the dead would be sufficient," she said, cool and dry, though he did not mistake that edge beneath it. "The media really is voracious these days."

"It depends on the story. Did you deliberately hide yourself away all this time? Or did you hit your head and forget who you were?" He kept his gaze trained on hers. "The former leads to all manner of unpleasant inquiries about why you might have felt it necessary to do such an irre-vocable thing and who might have been responsible. The latter, meanwhile, is a special interest story that will no doubt capture the public's interest for a while, as these things do, but will then fade away."

"So to be clear, we're not talking about the truth right now, despite how many times you've called me a liar in the past two weeks." She raised a challenging brow. "We're talking about manipulating the media for your own murky ends."

"No, Lily." His tone was harsh. He made no attempt to soften it. "We're talking about Arlo."

She looked shocked by that. "What does this have to do with Arlo?"

"He will eventually be able to read all about this," Rafael pointed out. "Assuming someone doesn't share the whole of it with him on a playground, as children are wont to do. It will be part of the very public story that he and anyone else can access at will. I'd prefer that story not be about his mother thinking so little of his father that she pretended to kill herself and then hid herself away for half a decade. What good could possibly come of his knowing that?"

Something glittered in that too-blue gaze of hers. "I'm not going to lie to him. I can't believe you'd really think I would."

"Please spare me the moral outrage. You've already lied to him. You've lied to everyone you've ever met, before and after that accident. At least this time, the lie would be in his best interests."

"You're assuming a lot," she said in a clipped tone, that glitter in her gaze even more hectic and a dark thing in her voice besides. "You barely know him. And one night with me after five years hardly gives you the right to make any kind of decision about what's in his best interests."

"I'm not assuming anything," Rafael said, soft and harsh, giving absolutely no quarter. "Arlo is my son. You either hid him away from me deliberately, in which case any court in the land is likely to award me custody in the face of such a contemptible parental act—or you didn't know what you were doing until I found you, which suggests a brain injury that hardly sets you up as mother of the year. I'd think long and hard about that, if I were you. I don't want to treat you like a business rival and take you down by any available means necessary. But if I have to, I will."

She eyed him as if she'd never seen him before and didn't much like what she saw now.

"Is that what last night was about?" There was no particular inflection in her voice, though he could see all manner of shadows in her gaze as she set her coffee back down on the nearby side table with a bit too much precision. "Trying to sneak your way beneath my defenses so you could better knock me flat today?"

"Lily." He said her name the way he heard it in his head, delicate and light, that same song that had been torturing him for all these years. "I have no reason whatsoever to think anything I did could reach you. Ever."

He saw her hands shake then, very slightly, before she clenched them into the fabric slipping and sliding around her. And it made him feel worse, not better. Hollow.

"So the fact it sounds a lot like you're threatening me is what, then?" she asked, her voice crisp, as if he'd imagined that small, telling tremor. "My overactive imagination? A remnant of that convent school poet you made up for your own amusement?"

"I wasn't threatening you. I'm merely pointing out the realities of the situation we find ourselves in."

"A man standing half-naked in a Venetian palazzo passed down through his family line for centuries maybe shouldn't set himself up as the last word on reality," she retorted. "It makes you sound silly." She lifted a hand when he started to respond to that. "I understand that your feelings are hurt, Rafael. That sex only made it all that much more raw, and maybe that much worse."

"You have no idea." He hadn't meant to say that. But he had, and so he thought he might as well keep going. "I want you, Lily. I can't deny that. It doesn't go anywhere, no matter how many times I lose myself in you. But that doesn't change what we did to each other. How we behaved and what came of it. As you said yourself last night."

"Neither does using my son—*our son*—as a weapon." She held his gaze. "What does that make you?"

"Determined," he retorted, a little more temper in his voice than he liked. As if he still had absolutely no control over himself where she was concerned. "I lost five years of his life. I won't lose a moment more."

"I haven't denied you access to him," she said stiffly. "I won't. We can work something out, I'm sure. People who can't manage to spend three seconds in a room together without drawing blood can do it. So can we."

"You're not understanding me." He waited for her to focus on him again. "There will be no split custody, no separate homes. He stays with me."

Lily's mouth actually dropped open. "You must have lost your mind."

"That leaves you with a very few options, I'm afraid, and I'm sorry for that," he said, and there was a part of him that hated that she'd gone pale, that this clearly surprised and hurt her. But not enough to stop. "You can stay with him, with me. But that will require we make this official—and while I won't pretend I'll manage to keep my hands off you, I can't promise I'll ever give you more than sex. I can't imagine I'll ever trust you." He shrugged as if that was of no matter to him. "Alternatively, you can go back to your life in Virginia or come up with a new one if you prefer, and you can call yourself any name you like until the end of time. But if you choose that option, you'll do so alone."

She didn't move, though he had the impression she swayed on her feet, and he wished this was different. He wished he could gather her in his arms, make her smile. Make all of this all right. But the saddest truth of all was that he didn't know how. Theirs was the high drama, the angst and the deeply thrust knife of betrayal. He didn't know how to make her smile. He only knew how to bring out the worst in her—and how to make her cry.

He'd done nothing but that, over and over again.

She's not the only one who needs forgiving, a tiny voice inside him suggested then, like a chill through his body. *There are monsters enough in both of you, more than enough to go around.*

But he didn't know how to stop this. How to fix it. How to save either one of them.

"I'm not leaving Arlo with you," she said, very precisely, as if she was worried she might scream if she didn't choose each word that carefully. "That will never happen, Rafael."

"My son will have my name, Lily," he warned her, yielding to his temper rather than that other voice that whispered things he didn't want to hear. "One way or another. You can be a part of this family or not, as you choose. But you're running out of time to decide."

"Running out of time?" She stared at him as if he'd

grown a monster's misshapen head as he stood there, and he wouldn't have been particularly surprised if he had. "Arlo didn't know you existed two weeks ago. You thought I was dead. You can't make these kind of ultimatums and expect me to take you seriously."

"Here's the thing, *cara*," he murmured, feeling that familiar kick of ruthlessness move in him, spreading out and taking over everything. It felt a lot like peace. He crossed his arms over his chest and told himself she was the enemy, like all the rivals he'd decimated in his years as acting CEO of the family business. He assured himself she was his to conquer as he chose. And more, that she'd earned it. "I'm sorry that this is hard for you. I feel for you, I do. But it won't change a thing."

Though it might have changed things if that glitter in her gaze had spilled over into tears. It might have reminded him that he could be merciful. That he really had loved her all along. But this was Lily, stubborn to the bitter end. She blinked, then again, and then those blue eyes were clear and hard as they met his. She tipped up that chin and she looked at him almost regally, as if there was nothing he could do to touch her, not really.

The same way she'd looked at him in that hallway when she was nineteen.

And he had the same riotous urge now as he had then: to prove that he damn well could. That he could do a great deal more than *touch* her. That he could mess her up but good.

He told himself that this time, at least, it was far healthier than it had been then, because it wasn't about either one of them. It was about their son.

Which was why he kept his distance. The way he hadn't done then.

And so what if it was killing him? That was the price. He assured himself Arlo was worth paying it.

"You have until Christmas," Rafael told her matter-of-factly. "Then you will either marry me or you'll get the hell out of my life, for good this time. And his."

CHAPTER TEN

"Have you decided what you'll do?" Rafael asked her the first morning after their somewhat subdued return from Venice later that frigid morning, smiling at her in that mocking way of his over the breakfast table. "The Dolomites themselves await your answer, I'm sure. As do I."

It was the feigned politeness, Lily thought, that made her want to fling the nearest plate of sausages at his head, if not at the mountains themselves. As if he was truly interested in her answer instead of merely needling her for his own amusement.

"Go to hell," she mouthed over Arlo's head, and only just managed to restrain herself from an inappropriate hand gesture to match.

But that only made his smile deepen.

It didn't help that Lily didn't know what she was going to do. There was no way she could ever leave Arlo, of course. Surely that went without saying. The very idea made her stomach cramp up in protest. But how could she marry Rafael? Especially when the kind of marriage he'd mentioned in Venice was a far cry indeed from the sort she'd imagined when she'd been young and silly and still thought things between them might work out one day.

Well, this was *one day*, and this was not at all what she'd call worked out, was it? This was, she was certain, pretty much the exact opposite of that.

"Perhaps we should make a list of pros and cons," he suggested on another afternoon even closer to Christmas, coming to stand beside her. She was on the warm and cozy side of the glass doors overlooking the garden, where Arlo and two of his nannies were building a legion of snowmen in what little gloomy light there was left at the tail end of the year. "Maybe a spreadsheet would help?"

Again, that courteous tone, as if she was deciding on nothing more pressing than which one of his wines she might choose to complement her dinner. It set her teeth on edge.

"Is this a game to you?" Lily asked him then, amazed that she could keep her voice so even when she wanted to take a swing at him. When she thought she might have, had that not involved touching him—which she knew better than to do, thank you. That way led only to madness and tears. Hers. "This isn't only my life we're talking about, you know. I get that you don't care about that. But it's Arlo's life, too, whom you do claim to care about, and you're messing with everything he holds dear."

She didn't expect him to touch her—much less reach over and take her chin in his hard hand, forcing her to look deep into his dark, dark eyes. Lily had to fight back that sweet, deep shudder that would have told him a thousand truths she didn't want him to know, and all of them things she'd already showed him in detail in that bed in Venice.

"We both made the choices that led us here," Rafael said softly, his hard fingers like a brand, blistering hot and something like delicious at once, damn him. "I can't help it if you don't like the way I'm handling the fallout, Lily. Do you have a better solution?"

"Anything would be a better solution!" she threw at him.

He dropped his hand, though he didn't step back for another jolting beat or two. That was her heart, she understood, not the world itself, though it was hard to tell the difference. She couldn't look at him—she couldn't bear it—so she directed her gaze out through the glass again instead, where the best thing they'd ever done together rolled a ball of snow that was bigger than he was across the snowy garden.

This is about Arlo, she reminded herself. *This is all about Arlo. Everything else that happens is secondary.*

"Name one, then," Rafael said, dark and too close. Daring her, she thought. Or begging her—but no. That wasn't Rafael. He didn't beg. "Name a better solution."

She shot him a look, then looked back toward their son. Their beautiful son, whom she'd loved hard and deep and forever since the moment she'd known he existed. Right there in that truck stop bathroom. She'd been terrified, certainly. And so alone. But she'd had Arlo and she'd loved him, long before she'd met him.

"You can think whatever you like," Lily said, low and fierce. "But none of the choices I made were easy. Not one of them. They all left scars."

"None of that changes where we are, does it?" he asked, his own voice quiet, and yet it still tore through her. "Our scars are of our own making, Lily. Each and every one of them. I find I can't forgive that, either."

Lily didn't answer him. And the next time she glanced over, he'd gone.

She told herself that was just as well.

And maybe it wasn't entirely surprising that the nightmares came back that night. And the next. And the night after that, too.

The screech of brakes, the sickening spin. That horrifying, stomach-dropping, chilling understanding that she wouldn't—*couldn't*—correct it. Then the impact that had thrown her from the car and left her sprawling, or so she'd pieced together afterward. She'd found herself face-down in the dirt, completely disoriented, scraped and raw in only a few places while around her, the northern California night had been quiet. A little bit foggy around the edges. Pretty, even, especially with the sea foaming over the rocks down below.

It hadn't been until the car had burst into flames some ways down the cliff that she'd realized what had happened. How close she'd come to death. How narrowly she'd escaped it, completely by accident.

Lily sat up too fast in her bed—again. This was, what? The fourth night in a row? Her heart was pounding so hard she thought it might punch a hole in her chest. The same way it had felt that night five years ago, when she'd finally comprehended what had happened. She'd almost forgotten the terror, all these years later. The insane *what if*s that had galloped through her head. The smell of brake fluid and burned rubber and that thick, choking smoke from the fire so real in her nose she took a few deep breaths before she understood it was a memory.

It had already happened. It wasn't happening now.

"It's only a dream," she whispered. "It isn't real."

Though the shadow that detached itself from the darkness near her doorway then was. It moved, it made her jaw drop—and then it was Rafael.

"What are you doing?" she gasped when she could speak, though she'd huddled up in a tiny ball against the ornate headboard. "You scared me!"

"That is going around," Rafael murmured.

He looked rumpled and irritable and something else she couldn't identify when he came to a stop beside her bed. She stared at him, the sight of his gorgeous body in nothing but a very low-riding pair of athletic trousers as soothing, oddly, as it was thrilling in the usual way. And his bare feet against the old carpet struck her as some kind of benediction.

"Rafael?" she asked, before that fire in her took over and made her do or say something she knew she'd regret. "What's the matter? What are you doing here?"

"You screamed," he said gruffly.

She swallowed, and took the time to uncurl her hands so they were no longer balled into fists. She felt cold, even under all of her blankets. And because she couldn't make sense of that—of his presence here. Had he come running?

"Oh," she said.

"Lily." There was none of that sharp politeness in his voice then. None of that mockery. And she couldn't see so much as a trace of either one on his face when he moved to the bedside table and snapped on the light. "Don't you think it's time you told me what happened that night?"

"That night?" she echoed, though she knew. Of course she knew. It was still reverberating in her head, still oozing around in the corners of the room. She frowned at him instead, because that was easier. "How did you hear me, anyway?"

"I have a gift," Rafael said, sounding dry and grumpy at once, which Lily realized was comforting, somehow. Though that made no sense. "I can hear two things with perfect clarity anywhere I go. The screams of terrified women, and irritating evasiveness at three twenty-seven in the morning."

He didn't reach for her, as she'd half expected. He leaned against the side of the bed, crossed his arms while he fixed that dark gaze of his on her, and waited.

And this was the story Lily had never told another living soul.

Maybe, she thought now, because he was the only person on earth who might understand what had happened and what she'd done—and she wasn't even sure about that. Not any longer.

"Are you sure you want me to tell you?" she asked him. "You've really been enjoying vilifying me. I'd hate to ruin that for you."

His dark eyes grew sterner and his jaw tightened, but he didn't say a word. He only waited—as if he could stand there all night, no matter what she threw at him.

Lily sighed and shoved her hair back from her face, moving to sit cross-legged there at the head of the bed. And then she'd run out of ways to stall. And he was so dark and so beautiful, and he was so wrapped up inside her that she felt him when she breathed in, and she'd never managed to get him out of her head or her heart. Not then. Certainly not now.

And she still didn't know what that made her. What that meant.

But it was the middle of the night. And the only light in the world seemed to fall in that tiny little circle from the side of her bed. She told herself it was the only confessional she'd be likely to get. And she took it.

Maybe all of this—from the moment he'd seen her on the street in Charlottesville all the way across the world to that night in Venice—had been leading them straight here. Maybe this had been the destination all along.

"You remember that last fight we had." She looked at him, then down at her hands, threading them together in her lap. It had been a long time ago, that fight. "In San Francisco that Thursday."

His sensual mouth flattened into a stern line. "I remember."

"It was the usual thing. I cried, you laughed. There

was that other woman you'd been in all the papers with. You dared me to leave you. I told you that this time I really would." Lily frowned at her fingers as she lifted one shoulder, then dropped it. "I didn't believe a word I said. Neither did you. We must have had that exact same fight a thousand times by then."

"More," Rafael agreed in that same too-dark voice, and she thought that was self-loathing she heard in his voice then. She recognized it. She'd heard it enough times in her own voice during those years.

"That weekend I went up to the château. It was a pretty night, I was bored and I was mad at you, so I helped myself to one of the overly fast cars in that absurd garage of your father's, and I took it for a drive." She lifted her head and looked at him. "I drove back down into the city. I wanted to see you."

She had the notion he was holding his breath. She pushed on.

"You weren't answering your phone, but I had a key to your house in Pacific Heights. I let myself in." She let out a sound that even she knew wasn't a laugh, but there was no helping it. This story was like an avalanche. Once it started, it rolled on and on until it wrecked everything. No wonder she'd never told it before. "I think I knew what was happening long before I made it to your bedroom. I don't remember hearing any sounds, but I must have—"

He swore. Deep and rich and inventively Italian.

"—because when I made it to your bedroom and looked inside, I wasn't as surprised as I should have been. If I hadn't had some warning, I mean. If I'd been surprised, I would have done something more than simply stand there, don't you think? Made a noise. Cried. Screamed. *Something*." She shook her head. "But I didn't."

"I don't know if it makes it better or worse," Rafael said

after a moment, as if it hurt him. As if he was speaking with someone else's voice, some stranger's voice that hadn't worked in years. "But I don't even remember her name."

Lily remembered far too much. She'd stared at the figures on the bed, willing them to not make sense, the way such things always failed to make sense in books. To be some kind of hectic blur—that would have been a blessing.

But she could see both of them, with perfect and horrifying clarity. She could still see both of them, burned forever into her brain.

Rafael had been deep inside a stunning brunette, and both of them had been breathing hard, getting closer and closer to a big finish. Lily had felt almost clinical for a moment, looking at them, because she'd known exactly what it felt like when Rafael did precisely what he'd been doing to that woman, and yet she'd been seeing it from a completely different angle…

The clinical thing hadn't lasted. It had fallen away, hard, and when it had gone Lily had felt sick.

"No," she said now. "I don't think that helps."

"Why didn't you say something?" he asked, his voice rough. "Then. As you stood there."

She eyed him. "Like what?"

He didn't answer that. Because what could she have said? What was there to say in such situations? Lily turned her attention back to her hands. She forced them to open, then clenched them again.

"It was one thing to know that you had other women. I always knew that. You didn't exactly make a secret of it. You even brought them home with you. But it was different to *see*."

She stopped to take a breath, and thought he almost said something—but he didn't. She hadn't asked him for forgiveness, Lily reminded herself. Maybe he wouldn't ask for any, either. Maybe there was no point bothering to apologize when wounds ran this deep. What was an apology between them, after all of this, but a pat little Band-Aid slapped over an amputated leg? What good would one do either one of them now?

What good does any of this do? some voice inside her demanded, but she couldn't stop now. She knew she couldn't.

"I didn't know what to do, so I turned around and I left," she told him. "As quietly as I'd come in. I walked out and stood there in front of your house. It was like an out-of-body experience. I kept thinking that at any moment, I'd start sobbing. That I would cry so hard and so long that it would rip me in half." She looked at him then. "But I didn't. I stood there a long time, but it never happened. So I got in the car again and I drove."

"Where were you going?" Rafael hardly sounded like himself, but Lily couldn't let herself worry about that. Not now. "To find your friends?"

"My friends hated you," she said and watched him blink as he took that in. "Oh, they didn't actually know it was *you*, but the secret man who always hurt me? They'd hated him for years. Openly. Any mention of you and it was all tough love and yelling. I didn't bother calling any of them. I knew what they'd say."

She shifted position, pulling her knees up beneath her chin. Rafael didn't move, standing there so still and so cold that Lily almost thought he'd turned himself into a statue.

"I just drove," she said. "Out of San Francisco and then out to the coast. I didn't have a plan. I wasn't sobbing or screaming or anything. I felt numb, really. But I knew what I was doing." She found his gaze in the dimly lit room, and imagined hers was no less tortured than his was. "I wasn't trying to hurt myself. You should know that."

"Then how did it happen?"

Lily shrugged. "I was going too fast in a too-powerful car. I took a turn and there was a rock in the middle of the road. I swerved, and then I couldn't correct it. I was skidding and there was nothing I could do about it."

She heard the brakes again, could hear her own swift curse so loud in the car's interior, and she remembered that stunned moment when she'd realized she really wasn't going to make it, she really wasn't going to save herself—

Lily shook it off and blew out a breath. "Then the car crashed. I don't remember that part. Only that I knew I was going to die." She swallowed, determined not to surrender to the emotion she could feel knocking around inside her. "But then I didn't. I was lying on the ground, not dead. I still don't know how."

"They think you went through the windshield," Rafael said, clipped and low. "That was the theory. From what was left of the car."

"Oh." She tried to picture it, but it made her feel dizzy again. Dizzy and fragile and entirely too breakable. "I guess that makes sense. I kind of came to on the shoulder, facedown in the dirt."

"You weren't hurt?"

He sounded so tense, she almost asked him if he was all right, but caught herself.

"I was shaken up," she told him. "I had some scrapes and was bleeding a little bit. The wind was knocked out of me. The bruises took a few days to really fully form and then a long time to fade." She hugged her knees closer to her. "But I was fine. Alarmingly fine, I thought, when the car blew up."

"Alarmingly?"

"I thought I was dead," she said simply. He went still

again. "It didn't make sense that I was...*fine*. The car was..."

"I know," he said harshly, his face in stark lines. "I saw it. It was mangled beyond recognition."

"How could anyone survive that?" Lily asked. "But then, when I tried to stand up, I got sick. And I figured dead people didn't throw up. I was pretty shaky." She braced herself for this next part and couldn't bring herself to look at him. She plucked at the blanket over her lap instead. "And then all I could think about was that I wanted you. I needed you."

She heard the sharp sound he made, but couldn't let herself analyze it or slow down. "I'd passed that town not far back, so I decided to walk back there and find a phone. I thought if I heard your voice, it would all be okay." Lily could still feel the heavy air that night, salt and wet, as the fog rolled in. She'd had dirt and blood in her mouth, and it had hurt a little bit to walk. But she'd kept going. "By the time I made it into town, the fire trucks were heading out. I don't know why I didn't flag them down. I think I was worried about the fact it was your father's car? And I didn't have permission to drive it. The whole walk to town, I kept thinking about how many hundreds of thousands of dollars I'd owe him and how I'd ever pay him back with a stupid degree in Anglo-Saxon elegies. It was on a loop in my head. I don't think I was thinking straight."

Rafael muttered something in Italian then, ragged and something like savage. But Lily kept going.

"I made it to a gas station and found a pay phone. Maybe the last working pay phone in California. And I picked it up to call you." She mimed picking up the phone, and she didn't know where that lump in her throat came from. That great pressure in her chest. She looked at him. She dropped her hand. "But what would have been the point?"

"Lily," he said, as if her name hurt him. He rubbed a hand over his jaw. But he didn't argue.

"Nothing was going to change," she said, almost as if he'd argued after all. He sat down hard on the end of the bed, then. His too-dark eyes were a torment, his mouth twisted, but she didn't look away. "It was this moment of awful clarity. You were in bed with that woman, but she could have been any woman and it could have been any given night. It didn't matter. It had been years and it was still the same. It wasn't going to change. *We* weren't going to change. And it was killing me, Rafael. It was *killing* me."

They sat there, separated by the length of the mattress and all of their history, for so long that if the sun had come up outside her windows Lily wouldn't have been at all surprised. But it was still dark when Rafael shifted position again. It was still dark when he cleared his throat.

And it told Lily everything she needed to know about how little she'd changed in all this time that she would have given absolutely anything to know what he was thinking then. She didn't even have the strength to call herself pathetic. It was simply that same old madness, all these years later. It was all the proof she needed that nothing was different. Herself least of all.

"What did you do then?" he asked.

"I told a nice Canadian couple at the gas station that my abusive boyfriend had left me there after a fight. They were so nice, they drove me all the way to Portland, Oregon, to get me away from him. When they kept going toward Vancouver, they left me at the bus station with cash and a ticket for my aunt's place in Texas."

"You don't have an aunt in Texas." His gaze moved over her face. "You don't have an aunt."

"No," she agreed. "But that was no reason not to go to Texas. So that was what I did. And then it was a week later, and everyone thought I was dead. No one even looked for me. So I decided I might as well stay dead."

"But you were pregnant."

She nodded. "Yes, though I didn't know that then."

"If you had?"

She wanted to lie to him, but didn't. "I don't know."

Rafael nodded once. Harshly, as if it hurt him. "And when you discovered that you were pregnant, it didn't occur to you a woman on the run, presumed dead, might not be the best parental figure for a child?"

"Of course it did," she said, frowning at him. "If I couldn't provide for him myself, I wasn't going to keep him. I had it all planned out."

"Adoption?" he asked, almost indifferently, though she didn't quite believe that tone of voice.

"No," she said. "You, Rafael. Of course, you. I figured I'd leave him on your doorstep or something. It seemed like a miracle that women hadn't already done that a hundred times, when I thought about it."

He absorbed that for a moment.

"But in no version of this story were you planning to come back," he said, when the silence began to feel much too thick between them. "Is that what I'm hearing?"

Lily hadn't expected that. She tried to read that closed-off look on his face, or the oddly stiff way he sat there at the foot of the bed. But either she'd lost her ability to see through him, or he was doing a far better job of hiding himself. She felt both possibilities as a loss.

"No, Rafael," she said quietly. "I wasn't coming back. Why would I?"

He met her gaze then, and she caught her breath. He looked haunted. Wrecked. She didn't understand why that made everything inside her seem to shatter like so much glass.

Lily wanted to go to him. She wanted to hold him, touch him—anything to make that terrible look on his face go away. Anything to make it better.

But she didn't move. She didn't dare.

"I can't think why you would," Rafael said into the dark, into what was left of the night. Straight into that heart of hers that Lily thought should have been healed by now, but was, she understood, still broken. "Not one single reason."

CHAPTER ELEVEN

RAFAEL FINALLY EMERGED from his offices on Christmas Eve, long after the sun went down and entirely lacking in anything approximating seasonal good cheer.

It had been years and it was still the same, Lily had said. *It wasn't going to change. We weren't going to change.*

He hadn't been able to get it out of his head since she'd said it. Tonight it was even worse. It had echoed inside his head, louder and louder, merging into some kind of ringing sound until he thought it might actually drive him mad. He'd been in his office, furiously working on projects no one would glance at until well into the new year, and he'd thought for a moment that he'd finally tipped over the edge into that madness that had so beguiled his own mother.

It had taken him long moments to realize that was not Lily's voice, but the sound of actual bells. Sleigh bells, if he was not mistaken, which had been curious enough to send him from his office and through the halls of the old house in search of the source.

He found his staff engaged in decking the old house even farther than they had already, despite the fact he'd informed them that his father and new bride would be in the Bahamas and Luca had decided to attend a house party abroad. And the decorating was being performed with significantly more enthusiasm than he recalled from previous years, which Rafael had no doubt had everything to do with the overexcited five-year-old who was all but turning somersaults in the grand front hall.

Rafael stood there, apart from the bustle down below. He leaned on the railing from the floor above and looked down at servants he'd never seen smile in all his life beaming at his son.

His son.

Arlo, who was like sunlight. Arlo, who emanated sheer joy like a homing beacon.

Arlo, whose mother had hated Rafael—or had despaired of him, and Rafael couldn't say he'd been able to discern the difference—so much that she'd gone to tremendous, all but unimaginable lengths to get the hell away from him. She'd walked away from a horrific car crash. She'd hitchhiked out of state. She'd found herself pregnant and penniless, and even then her plans had centered around what might be best for the baby, but never, not once, had she considered returning to Rafael.

And he couldn't argue about a single point in that story she'd finally told him. He'd been in that bed, with that nameless, faceless woman, not that he'd imagined for a moment that Lily might have seen him. He'd been the man Lily had described in every regard—the one who'd laughed at her, cheated on her though he'd claimed they had no formal commitment, and he had always, always assumed she'd come back to him.

How had he convinced himself that if she'd lived, she'd have been his? When he'd done everything in his power back then to make sure they would never, ever be together?

Lily had decided that she'd rather let everyone she knew think she was dead than play those terrible games any longer, and Rafael couldn't blame her. It was time he told her that, he thought then, watching his son laugh and jump up and down on the floor below. He had no business making ultimatums when the truth was, he was the one who ought to—

"How nice of you to emerge from your cave at last." Rafael turned slowly at the sound of that bone-dry voice. Lily stood in the gallery that functioned as a kind of upper-story foyer in this part of the house, her arms crossed over her chest and a scowl on her face. "The self-flagellation cave, presumably. I was beginning to think we'd have to break you out with dynamite. I was leaning toward throwing some at your head."

Rafael blinked. "I beg your pardon?"

Her scowl deepened, and he couldn't help but feel that like any other woman's sexiest come-hither glance. It slid along his spine and pooled in his groin, licking him with the sweet flame of it. She was wearing nothing but a pair of loose trousers and a soft, dark sweater, with all of her hair piled up on the top of her head, and still, he wanted her. Deeply. Utterly. Desperately.

The more she scowled at him, the more he wanted her. And the more he hated himself for it.

"Arlo thinks you've been sick," Lily told him, sounding unaccountably furious. "Because guess what, Rafael? When you're a parent, you don't get to flounce off whenever you feel like it and lie about like an opera heroine until you feel like coming back. You're a father all of the time, not just when it's convenient."

He'd spent more than forty-eight hours wrestling with his guilt, his shame and all the self-loathing that went with it, and it turned out two seconds in Lily's company was all it took to slice right through it. He tilted his head to one side and narrowed his gaze as he looked at her.

"Am I Arlo's parent, Lily?" he asked coolly. "Because I

was under the impression that, blood tests aside, you had no intention of telling that boy who his father is."

"I could have told him the entire history of the Castelli family over the past two days," she fired back at him. "A hundred times over. And you wouldn't know either way, because you've been locked up in your office feeling sorry for yourself."

"I wasn't feeling sorry for myself," he grated at her. "I was feeling sorry for you. For having put you through this in the first place."

That came out a little too rough and shimmered there between them, entirely too honest. Bald and naked in the shadows of the gallery where they stood.

"Well," she said, her voice a little less sharp than it had been a moment before. "There's no need to retrace those steps. I did that for years. It doesn't actually help."

"Lily…" But he didn't know how to say what needed to be said.

Her eyes were too bright suddenly, and that scowl of hers seemed fiercer and more precarious at once. "And you know what else doesn't help? You demanding the truth and then running away when you get it, leaving me to deal with it. Again."

"I am every last thing you accused me of being," he said then. "More. There's no pretending otherwise."

"That's very noble, of course," she threw at him. "But that doesn't change the fact that we have a son, and he doesn't care if you've just discovered that the great and epic love story you've been holding onto for all these years is a sham."

"Don't." He didn't mean to growl that at her. "Don't say that."

Her eyes were still too bright and much too dark at once.

"Come on, Rafael," she said quietly, though there was

that edgy thing in her voice, and the way she held herself, like broken glass that would never fit together again. "You know better. This was nothing more than sex and secrecy. Two kids playing games with dangerous and unforeseen consequences, nothing more."

"You don't believe that." He shook his head when she started to speak. "If you did, you never would have run away. You certainly wouldn't have raised Arlo on your own. 'Two kids playing games' isn't a good enough reason for a deception of that magnitude, Lily, and you know it."

She looked brittle in the mellow light, but that didn't make her any less beautiful.

"I don't want to marry you," she told him, and there was something in her voice then that pierced straight through him, as if she'd broken apart where she stood. But she hadn't. He could see she stood proud and tall, the way she always had. Maybe he was the one who was broken. "And I'm not leaving Arlo here with you and going off somewhere. I would tell you what I think you can do with your ultimatum, but you've already spent days brooding in your office. God knows what it would do to you if I really let loose."

He studied her for a moment, while Arlo's high-pitched voice, nearly a soprano tonight with all his excitement, echoed all around them. And this was wrong. He felt that, deep inside. This was all wrong. But he shoved his hands in his pockets instead of touching her the way he wanted to do.

He told himself that was what a good man would do. And once—just once—he would be the good man for her he'd never been when it counted.

"Consider the plane at your disposal," he told her, and he thought he saw her shoulders sag, slightly, as if she'd wanted—but that was wishful thinking, and a second later, he was sure he'd imagined it. "It can take you wherever you want to go. I won't fight you for custody. As you said before, all kinds of people figure out visitation. I'm sure we will, too."

"I'm sure we will." Lily's voice was hollow. "How civilized, Rafael. I wouldn't have thought we had it in us."

And this time when she walked away from him, Rafael let her go.

Lily tried to sleep.

Arlo was so fired up about Christmas that he'd inevitably had a complete and total meltdown and ended up sprawled out on her bed in an exhausted heap of five-year-old tears. Lily had soothed him as best she could when the issue was too much sugar and the sheer injustice of it *still* not being Christmas morning until he'd finally fallen asleep. She'd crawled into bed beside him, flipped open a book and told herself that this was perfect. That this was the life she'd had for the past five years and it was the life she wanted. Her little boy and the little life they led together, somewhere far away from here. From Rafael. Books and dogs and absolute and total freedom. What could be better?

But she hadn't been able to make any sense at all out of the words on the page before her, no matter how many times she reread the sentences. Eventually she'd given up. She'd cuddled Arlo's flushed little-boy body next to hers and she'd shut her eyes tight, confident that she would drift off into sleep immediately.

Instead, she lay awake, glaring at the ceiling of this old house, growing more and more furious by the minute. And the more she tried to keep herself from tossing and turning, the worse it got.

It was after midnight when she finally gave up. She

climbed out of the bed, taking care to tuck Arlo back in. She shoved her feet into her warm slippers and she wrapped a long sweater around her like a robe, and she found herself out in the dark, cold hallway before she could think better of it.

She made her way down the main stairs, where the Christmas decorations looked stately and quiet in the dimness. She stood there for a moment, at the foot of the stairs, but then whatever demon had spurred her out of bed kept her going. She found herself at the doors to the main library before she could talk herself out of it.

The room was a showpiece. The jewel of the house, she'd heard Rafael's father say once. It was a huge library filled with floor-to-ceiling shelves accessed with the kind of rolling stairs and ladders that made Lily giddy with a book lover's joy, though this was the kind of library that featured books that were better looked at than read. This time of year, that hardly mattered, as the huge Christmas tree dominated the far end of the room, where there was normally a larger sitting area done up in pompous leather chairs and blocky masculine accessories.

And tonight, Rafael stood at the fireplace, one arm braced on the mantel above it, his face toward the flames.

Lily stood there in the doorway for a moment, letting that great, yawning thing that was all her many and complicated feelings for this man take her over. It washed through her, buffeting her like a riptide, turning her over and over and over until she could hardly see straight.

Until she focused on Rafael, that was, and he was all she could see.

Maybe, she thought, it had always been that way for a reason. Maybe she wasn't sick or twisted. Maybe they'd simply been too young to handle what had been there between them from the very start.

Maybe.

She was so damned tired of all these *maybe*s.

"You did it again," she said, and her voice sounded reedy and strange in the vastness of this formal, stuffy room. By the fire, Rafael didn't move. It made her think he'd known she was there, and something curled up deep inside her at the thought. "You ran away. Right there in plain sight. You used to do it with other women. Tonight you did it with your supposed self-loathing and your noble gestures no one asked you to make. But it was still running away, wasn't it?"

"I suppose we could have a competition to see who gets farther," he replied after a moment, but at least his voice was dark and low again. Not that strained, polite voice he'd been using earlier tonight. At least here and now he sounded like *Rafael* again. He looked at her then, without straightening. "Have you packed, then? Or are you planning to walk back to Virginia as you are?"

The unfairness of that felt like another great wave crashing over her head, and the smart move would have been to turn around and leave—but she didn't. Instead, Lily took another step into the room.

"What would it matter if I did or didn't?" she demanded. "You don't care either way."

"I care." His voice was a lash across the firelit room. "Believe whatever you must, but know that. *I care.*"

He straightened then, and it took her a moment to truly appreciate how disreputable he looked at the moment. Gone were the tailored suits, the casually elegant daywear. This version of Rafael seemed a good deal more... raw. His shirt was open, potentially misbuttoned. She didn't think he'd shaved recently. And that look in his dark gaze...burned.

Lily still didn't leave. She studied him for a moment

while too many emotions battled it out inside her. Too many to count. Too many to name.

"You've convinced yourself that this is all some great love story, haven't you?" she demanded. "It wasn't."

"No?" he asked, and he roamed toward her then, that stark, dangerous expression on her face thrilling her in a way she told herself she didn't understand. But her body did, the way it always did. It flushed hot, then melted. Everywhere. "It should have been."

"Things are only epic to you when you've lost them, Rafael, have you noticed that?" She didn't know what made her more furious—him, or her body's response to him, which had only intensified. If anything, that night in Venice had made it worse. "This can only be a love story if I leave you. That's what you want."

"I love you." It was harsh and flat, and they both stared at each other as it hung there between them, dancing like an errant spark from the fire on the old rug, then disappearing. She thought he would take it back, but instead, he breathed deep and held her gaze. "I should have told you then. I should have told you every day since I found you again. I should have told you tonight. I love you, Lily."

Lily stared back at him, stunned. Scraped through and emptied out. But then another wave hit, this one harder than the ones before, and she laughed. It was an ugly sound. She heard the harshness of it echo back to her, but she couldn't stop. She couldn't make it stop, not even when Rafael drew closer and stood there above her.

"Stop," he said, and he made it worse with that look on his face, something like gentle, and the way his hard mouth softened. It nearly did her in. She jabbed at her eyes with hands that had turned into fists without her noticing. "You don't need to do this."

"Love doesn't *do* anything, Rafael," she threw at him

then. "It doesn't save anyone. It can't change anything. It's an excuse. A catchall. In the end, it's meaningless. And, at its worst, destructive."

He reached over and slid his hand around the side of her neck, holding his palm there. Over her pulse, she realized. As if he was checking in with her heart—and that, too, made everything inside her seem to lurch and then slide. She was finding it hard to stay on her feet.

But she couldn't look away from him, either.

"You're talking about what people do with love, or in its name," he said. "But that's people. Love is bigger and better than all those things."

Lily shook her head. "How would you know? My mother's shining example? Or maybe your father's?"

She wanted to jerk her head away from him, knock his hand off her. But she didn't, and she couldn't have said why. Only that it was connected to that trembling knot inside her that seemed to get harder and bigger the more it shook.

"They're people," Rafael said. "Flawed and limited, like anyone."

"My mother spent her life chasing the next high. Men. Drugs. Whatever. Your father gets married for sport. You call those flaws? I'd call it something more like pathological."

"Are you and I any better?" Rafael asked, and he couldn't know, she thought, how much the heat of his hand warmed her. How much she wanted to simply topple into it and let him hold her there forever… He couldn't possibly know that, could he?

"That's my point." Her voice was little more than a whisper. "I told you the truth and you wanted nothing to do with me. I told you I'd take your child away from you again and you'd let me do it. You and I are *worse* than our parents, Rafael. We're much, much worse."

He shifted then, bringing his other hand up to hold her on the other side and tipping her face toward his.

"No," he said, in his uncompromising way. So certain. So ruthlessly *sure*. "We are not."

But she was warming to her theme, to that knotted thing inside her, as if it might choke her if she didn't get all of this out.

"And what I don't understand is what it's all for," she threw at him. "What's the point? The things you did or I did, then or now. The things anyone does. What is there to show for any of it?"

"You," Rafael said. "Me. Arlo." He shrugged in that way of his, Italian and uncompromisingly male, his dark eyes fixed to hers. "This is what love is. This is what *life* is. Complicated. Brutal. Glorious." His hands tightened and he drew her closer, until they stood in what was nearly a kiss. Nearly. "Ours, Lily. This is *ours*."

"Rafael…"

"I will put you on that plane myself," he gritted out. "If that's what you want. If you really want to put this— *me*—behind you."

And she opened her mouth to tell him that was exactly what she wanted, but didn't. She couldn't, somehow. It all whirled around inside her. All the fear, the pain. The running and the hiding across all these years. The lies, then and now. Had she cut herself off from her life because of Rafael? Or had Rafael been the last strike in a life spent coming a distant second to whatever her mother was losing herself in that month?

Maybe, just maybe, it was all the same running away.

And maybe it was finally time she stopped.

She'd never stopped loving this man. She'd simply never learned how to do it without losing everything in the process. Her life. *Herself.*

"And if I don't?" she dared to ask, if softly. "If I don't want that?"

Rafael studied her face for a long, long time. So long that Lily forgot everything except the stark male beauty of his face. So long that she forgot herself, too, all those dark things that crowded their past, and smiled up at him with every last bit of that shaking, knotted thing inside her that she was very much afraid was hope.

And it was worth everything, she thought, to see that answering curve take over his face, transforming him before her eyes from that grim, hard man to the Rafael she'd loved before she'd known she shouldn't. The Rafael who had been so beautiful to a sixteen-year-old girl that she hadn't dared to look at him directly.

As if she'd known even then that once she did, she'd never look away.

"I want to make you smile, Lily. I want to make you happy." His mouth brushed hers, a smile to a smile, and made her shiver deep inside. "But I don't have the slightest idea how to do that."

So she wrapped her arms around his neck and she pulled him close, resting her forehead against his.

"Love me," she said, all of that emotion making her voice thick and her knees feel weak in turn. "I think that's a good start."

"I always have," he told her, his words resonating like a vow. "I always will."

She breathed in deep, then breathed out all the dark and the pain, the hurt and the fury. She let it go, like snow into the water of those dark Venice canals.

"Rafael," she whispered, "I've been in love with you all my life. I wouldn't know how to go about stopping. I never have. I don't think I ever will."

"I'll make sure of it," he promised her.

And Lily didn't know if he kissed her or she kissed him, only that they came together and this time, she felt that knotted thing open up, hope like light inside her and inside him, flooding them both. Love. Life. Complicated and wonderful—and for the first time in her life, she truly believed she could have all of those things. With him. Finally, with him.

Rafael lifted her up into his arms and carried her across the room. Then he laid her down beneath the sparkling lights of the first Christmas tree that was truly theirs, on the very first day of the rest of their lives, and started working on forever.

Kiss by perfect kiss.

CHAPTER TWELVE

THE FOLLOWING YEAR Arlo was his parents' only attendant in their Christmas wedding, there in the chapel in the woods near the grand old house by the lake, in the shadow of those towering Italian mountains that felt like eternity.

"I have something to tell you," Rafael had told his son that first Christmas morning together, after the little boy had lost himself in a frenzy of gifts and wrapping paper and subsided to playing with his current favorite video game. That day.

"Is it about cake?" Arlo had asked without setting the game aside. "I like cake. Yellow cake, but chocolate is okay."

"No," Rafael had said, wondering how it had been possible to feel that awkward and yet that *right* at the same time. "I wanted to tell you that I'm your father."

Lily had been sitting there on the couch, pretending not to listen. She'd been doing it loudly.

Arlo had seemed preoccupied with his game. Then he'd asked, "Forever?" after considering the matter.

"Yes," Rafael had told him solemnly. "Forever. That's how it works."

"Cool," Arlo had said, and that had been that.

His mother had been a different matter.

Rafael gazed at her now as she took one of Arlo's hands

and he took the other. They smiled at each other as they walked toward the priest who waited for them at the small altar.

"Marry me because you want to," he'd said as Christmas gave way into the brand-new year. They were still together. They were filled with that half hope, half certainty that their complicated past meant they'd already weathered the worst storms anyone could. "Not because I told you to."

"Because your son must have your name?" she'd replied lightly, with that teasing glint in her blue eyes but, he thought, something more serious beneath it.

"My son *will* have my name," Rafael had assured her, every inch of him the powerful head of his family's fortune. And the man who loved them both. "It is only a question of when."

But it turned out Lily thought there was some ground to cover first.

There was the issue of her resurrection, first and foremost. For Arlo's sake, they decided to say she'd had amnesia all these years. That running into Rafael on the street had jolted her back to herself.

"And in a way," Lily told him one night as they lay tangled together in his house in San Francisco, "that's even true."

"It's the kinder story to tell," Rafael had agreed, smoothing a hand down the length of her lovely back. "For all of us."

She'd fielded questions from all sides, and not all of it the media. Her old friends, who'd mourned her death and now wanted nothing but to bask in her return. All the various parts of the life she'd left behind and found so different now that she'd come back to it. She'd discovered her time running Pepper's kennels gave her rather more managerial skills than she'd imagined they might, and when a position came up at the Castelli Wine corporate office in Sonoma, she took it. She'd visited her mother's grave and told Rafael that she found some comfort in knowing that the woman was finally at peace.

But it was dealing with his family that she was the most worried about, he knew.

It helped, Rafael thought, that they'd already had a son. There was no hoping the family would get used to the idea—there was a little boy who didn't care whom his grandparents had been married to before his birth.

And after the initial shock, Gianni Castelli had shrugged in a rueful way of his that reminded Rafael of when his father had been a younger man. The child bride—Corinna—had been having a loud conversation on her mobile phone out in the abundant sunshine that danced through the cypress trees at the Sonoma Valley château, and Gianni had gazed at her fondly before turning his gaze back to his son.

"Love levels every one of us, one way or another," he said. "It helps if you don't brace yourself against the fall. You're more likely to break something that way. Better by far to let gravity do what it will. It will anyway."

Luca, of course, had merely laughed. Then clapped Rafael on the back, hard. Then laughed again, but that time, Rafael had laughed with him.

Lily reconnected with Pepper under her real name, and even tracked down the sweet Canadian couple who had spirited her out of California that fateful night, finally able to pay them back for their kindness to her.

And then, on an autumn day in the south of France where they'd flown for a wine show, she'd finally agreed to marry him.

"I don't know what took you so long," Rafael said gruffly.

"Because," she said fiercely, stopping dead in the middle of a bustling market in Nice to look up at him solemnly, "I wanted to be sure this time."

He'd been unable to keep himself from touching her. He hadn't tried. "That I wouldn't run away?"

"That *I* wouldn't," she said softly, and she smiled up at him, her strawberry blond hair like a halo in the fine French light. "And I won't, Rafael. Not ever again."

And so at last they stood there in the small chapel and recited their vows, to each other and for their son. When they were finally husband and wife, they walked back to the house while Arlo ran on ahead, pressing their shoulders together the way they had long ago. Inside, the rest of the family waited to join in the celebration and tip it straight into Christmas, but first, Rafael stopped her at the door before she would have gone in.

It was cold, but when he held out his hand, palm facing her, she met it with hers.

This was who they were. This heat. This connection. It had defied their scandalous beginnings, the possibility of death and far too many lies. It had endured when they didn't trust each other at all, and while they'd taught each other how to smile.

"All the rest of our days," Rafael said. "*Mi appartieni.*"

"And you belong to me," Lily agreed, the glimmer of tears in her gorgeous blue eyes. "Forever."

And then he took her hand in his, his wife at last, and led them safely home.

* * * * *

*If you loved Rafael's story,
you won't want to miss his brother Luca's!
CASTELLI'S VIRGIN WIDOW
by Caitlin Crews
Available in February 2016!*